Nicole,

Stealing Ryder

By: V. Murphy

Thanks for reading & joining Harper and Ryder on their adventure.

XOXO ♥ V

ISBN-13: 978-1493718283

ISBN-10: 1493718282

SEQUEL WARNING: STOP BEFORE CONTINUING READING! This is book 2 of a series. If you have not read Sharing Harper, please go do so before continuing with Stealing Ryder.
Thanks,
V

Cover Models: Erin McPartlin & Bryan Kennard
Author Photo: Cal Connolly
Edited by Kayla Robichaux AKA Kayla the Bibliophile
Formatting by Danielle Jamie

Praise for *Sharing Harper*

"The chemistry between Ryder and Harper had me fanning myself. Seriously!!" –*HEA Book Shelf*

"The drama that came with this story. I am a drama JUNKIE!!" – *Crystal's Many Reviewers*

"We give miss V the up-most respect for broaching this real topic that, affect millions of people around the world on a daily basis." – *Scandalous Book Blog*

"This book was one of the best I have read so far this year." –*Rose's Book Blog*

"GREATEST BOOK I HAVE READ ALL WEEK!! V. Murphy you nailed this one on the head!!" – *2 Chicks and a Blog*

CONTENTS

To all those who supported my dreams, this is for you.
For my VIP girls.

A special dedication to my someone special who is currently overseas deployed. You cannot imagine how proud I am of you, JT.
Come home safe & sound.
Thank you for being my very own Ryder.
I love you.
- V

"I am not what happened to me, I am what I choose to become."
- Carl Gustav Jung

Chapter 1

One month later

Ryder

The sun crept into the room, and all I did was stare at the curvature of her beautiful back pressed tightly against mine. The slow breaths she took calmed me. When I couldn't sleep, I would sit up all night, staring at her tanned skin, flowing brown hair, and the curve that etched between her tits and her hips, dipping in and exposin' her small waist. I was taken back to where her smile spread from ear-to–ear, and the dimples on her cheeks were adorable and sexy in the same way. I needed her to move her little body around mine all day. We'd eat take-out and pizza, and she'd fuck me senseless at night, until her legs buckled beneath her and my cock was in pain.

I didn't need anything more than what I already had right now.

Durin' the day, we would deal with work, but nights were consumed with each other. I couldn't get enough of her. I was desperate, selfish, and always needed more of her. She was mine, only mine. I just wanted to spoil her, as she deserved to be spoiled.

If I ever said out loud what finding Harper meant to me, the guys would mock the soft spot I have for that woman. They didn't know how it felt to have a woman so attuned to my desires; and I'm not just talking sex. It may sound cheesy, but meetin' Harper was the second most important day in my life, the first being the day Evelyn was born. I remember it like it was yesterday.

"When is this thing going to be over?" I grumbled under my breath, but still continued waiting patiently, giving her the support she needed to get through the unbearable pain. I kept runnin' back and forth, grabbin' her ice cubes to suck on and cold rags for her head, because that's what those stupid mommy books said to do. I wish I had read more of those damn things…

I sat there, just looking at her and thinkin' that through the months of torture, today was the day I was going to meet my daughter; she's the one thing I could finally be proud of in my life.

Today would also be the day I vowed to change everything I had done wrong. To stop being that dumbass college kid and become a damn father. I would never turn out like my own father, and do everything opposite of his asshole unsupportive self.

Hours and hours passed, and once we hit the 24 hour mark, I started to feel faint myself. After forever, and pushes assisted by one doctor and a flurry of nurses, this beautiful child came out, and I was in shock. My heart expanded with love, and an unexplainable feeling shot through my chest.

She flew out screamin' and kickin'; the moment I got to see her, I spotted her bright blue eyes that were shaped the same as mine, and the full head of dark black hair that matched. From that second on, she was a part of me; she was my reason to wake up in the morning, and my reason to breathe. It was powerful in an unexplainable sort of way.

The rustling of the sheets caught my attention just as the sun shone through the windows. Since Harper and I became involved, I haven't left her once in the morning without telling her goodbye, ever since the day I left her stranded alone at the hotel. That entailed waking her up early, but I had to. I wanted to fuckin' punch myself for being a crass idiot and leaving her that morning, but I knew I had to go before the ocean got too crowded with other dudes.

"Hey, beautiful," I whispered in her ear, while slowly biting down on her lobe and kissing her neck. This woman was so sexy, and I loved making her groan with pleasure, which is exactly what she did.

Her body shifted as she turned around to face me. Her small button nose and lush lips sent me into a tailspin. Her hair was messed around her face, and when she blinked, she greeted me with her large brown eyes. They mesmerized me and invited me in.

"Mhmmm," she groaned, and her hands came up to touch my chest. She had the smoothest, little fuckin' hands around. I clenched my abs when she touched me, shivering from her cold little fingers. I imagined them caressing me, makin' me beg her for more. I pictured the warm wetness of her mouth circling the tip of me, and instantly went hard. Fuck, I was going to have to walk this off before I could get dressed.

"I will never get used to these hot-ass abs," she murmured through sleepy yawns.

"Go back to sleep, babe. I am goin' to go surf for a little bit. I will be back in a few hours," I whispered, hoping she wouldn't try to move towards me any further. I couldn't control my sexual appetite around her; but I had to get out on the ocean, and I knew if she were to try anything else, it would be the end of me.

"Okay," she breathed.

She was exhausted, and needed her sleep now. "I'll miss you," she said, and planted her sexy lips against mine, sending my cock into a painful realization that it wasn't going to taste the inside of her until later.

"I love you, Harper Mae." I gave her the lightest kiss against her forehead, just as she curled back into the comforter and fell asleep with a smile plastered on her face.

I got up to get dressed, and threw some shit into a bag. I never missed a day of surfing; it was my release from life's crap. I felt alone yet invigorated when I was ridin' the waves. It was almost the same feeling I had when I was on the football field…almost. I grabbed my wetsuit from the closet, and threw my board in the back of my Ford pickup.

As I drove down the island and towards the local surfing spot, I watched the sun rise from the east. I was content with the life I had now. Somehow, though, something was missing, and I had a feeling it had to do with family. There was still a part of me that wanted to mend things with my family and Kylee.

I dreaded going to pick up Evelyn every other day because Kylee's comments towards me were pissin' me off. She didn't want to see me happy with Harper or moved on, and she had to find her place. She wanted me for herself, just like she always had. That was never going to happen. She had to back off before I forced her off.

After I finished this surf session, it was going to be hard to go to the house to pick up Evelyn; but I had to remind myself that I was doing this for my daughter. Everything I did now was for Evelyn and Harper. They would be the only girls in my life.

***

I pulled into the parking spot, slipped on the rest of the wetsuit, and grabbed my board from the truck. I saw a couple guys I knew and joined them as we paddled into the ocean. When we reached our spot, we sat there waiting for the right wave.

The water lapped as we bobbed up and down with each passing bump. The sounds of the crashin' ocean at the shore and the seagulls above us calmed my nerves, which always peaked when I knew I was about to ride a wave.

"Yo, Ry, did you read about that surf competition coming up in October?" a buddy of mine, Finn, asked.

"Yeah, the big one with ESPN?"

"Yeah! You goin' to enter?"

I thought about this for a second; I had never actually competed in surfing. A couple guys on the ocean marveled at how fast I was able to pick the sport up.

After my football injury, my body wanted to stay active; so I figured, since I was in San Diego, I might as well try it. I took a couple lessons from Finn, and that's how we bonded and started hanging out.

"I don't know, man. Pat keeps tellin' me I should, but I don't think I am good enough." Pat was my old football agent. He said it would be good to enter somethin' and get my career started again, this time maybe in surfing.

"Do it! You're totally good enough, man. Plus, you still have a whole month to decide if you want to do it anyways."

"Are you enterin'?" I asked, my southern accent heavily emphasized.

"For sure, dude!" He beamed. Finn was your very typical "brah." Blonde hair, tan skin, the total California "hottie" as Skye would say. He didn't have a full time job; instead, he worked as a bartender at one of the local clubs. Even though he worked until 2am sometimes, he was always out on Coronado at 4 or 5 am. "Let's hit this wave," he echoed over the crash of the ocean.

The wave was large enough, and didn't show any prediction of closing anytime soon. We both paddled forward and braced as the wave came up from behind us. As the wave broke, we split up. Finn went for the right side and I braced left. Just as the wave reached it's largest point, I stood up, briefly hobblin' to regain balance. As I grasped my balance, I pulled up and rode the wave out. I allowed it to swallow me as I weaved in and out, riding along the inside of the closing tunnel. I spun twice on the board, moving up and down because the wave closed and I reached the shore. It was a damn good feelin' to pull into shore in one piece.

I looked over to the right where Finn was, and realize he didn't ride the wave out. He was waving his hand at me, gesturing to swim towards him.

I grabbed my board out from under me and started paddling towards him.

"Dude! Sick ride," he exclaimed when I was close enough to hear him.

"It wasn't that big," I hesitated. I wasn't one to boast about my athletic abilities. In fact, many of the guys didn't even know I used to play for the NFL. Finn only knows because one drunken night I confessed it to him.

"I am totally going to talk to Patrick about putting you in the competition in October. Can't say no."

"I'll think about it." I laughed knowing I wasn't prepared at all for the competition. Hell, I was just a beginner; sure, I had the strength, but I didn't have the experience.

"Whatever you say man," Finn said, as he began swimming out towards the ocean. "You wanna go to the bar Monday? Bring Harper and her hot, unavailable friend?"

"Yeah, sounds good. I'll run it by Harper, but I am sure we can meet you there around 10 pm?" I called back.

"Sounds rad."

"You know Skye is engaged right?" I reminded him.

"Yeah dude, but just cause there is a goalie doesn't mean you can't score." He busted up laughing, and I fist pumped him before paddling the other way.

"Hey man, I got to go pick up Evelyn, but I'll catch ya' later," I drawled, as I started paddling back to shore.

"October, bro!" Finn screamed at me as the breaking waves started pushing me out more towards the shore. When I finally reached the shore, I pulled myself off the board and gathered the rest of my stuff on the beach. I threw the board back in the truck and started it up. I drove through Coronado, and onto the bridge that connected the island to the mainland. I drove the same path I always took, down the I-5.

Today's drive was different. I haven't said anything to Harper, but Kylee threatened to move back to Texas the other day. She told me she was miserable here, and had trouble making friends. With her bitchy-ass attitude, I was not surprised, but I couldn't leave Evelyn in Texas. It was not going to happen, ever.

If Kylee took off with Evelyn, then I would have to follow. I couldn't even imagine the thought of leaving Harper; but I knew she wanted to be here for her best friend, Skye's wedding, and to finish her last year at school. So I haven't brought it up with her…yet.

I pulled up to the cottage Kylee rented in the suburbs. Kylee came from old money, but she spent it on Evelyn. She wasn't a bad mother at all; she just keeps insisting on this bullshit about gettin' together, which ain't gonna happen. A relationship we never had and never will have. As much as I would have loved to work something out with her, Harper was, and always will be, my life. I learned how to breathe again with Harper around me. If only Kylee would finally understand. I didn't love her; my entire heart belonged to Harper.

I pulled up and parked the truck in the driveway. I hope to God this is not be the last time I come around. Hell no, my child will not be sent to Texas away from me. I respected Kylee and all, so I certainly don't wanna be draggin' her to court. I just wanted a relationship with my daughter, and I don't get where Kylee is coming from, wantin' to take that all away from me. I opened the truck door and prepared myself for hell.

When I saw her come up from inside the house, a devilish grin formed on her face. She slid up next to me before I could even step through the threshold.

"I missed you so much," she murmured in my ear, while moving her hands along the tops of my arms, which were still wet from the ocean.

"Stop it now, Kylee," I commanded with force, but not before I looked around to make sure Evelyn hadn't run out.

"What's the problem, baby? That stupid girl of yours got you on a tight leash? She's a fucking bitch," Kylee spat in my face.

I lowered my voice and stared her straight in the eyes without shifting once. That would be the last time she ever said something like that about Harper. Coming from her, she sounds heartless as fuck. Harper was constantly worried about Kylee hating her, and always making sure I asked Kylee's permission before she saw Evelyn. While Kylee was always hesitant about Harper, her hatred for her was new.

"I know you're scared, Kylee, and I know I hurt you, but I swear to you, if you ever call Harper a bitch or anything along those same lines again, I will make your life hell. Hell, do you understand that?" My voice was low, but echoed determination and anger.

"Whatever, Ry. You and I both know she isn't the right girl for you anyways."

I pushed past her, not even acknowledging her statement. As I walked into the living room, I saw Evelyn playing with one of her numerous Barbie doll sets. I smiled, remembering the many times I've played prince to her princess; because while the guys I used to play football with would laugh at that sight, I treasured the moments I could protect little Evelyn from the evils of the world. She would always be Daddy's little girl in my eyes.

"Hey princess, you ready to go to Daddy's house?" I asked the very distracted little girl.

"Daddy!" she exclaimed in the small yet high-pitched voice of hers.

She ran up to where I was standing. When she reached me, I reached down to her and whisked her up to my chest, where she nuzzled into my neck.

"I love you so much, princess," I whispered in her ear.

Kylee, who was standing behind us, coughed to interrupt.

"Go grab your bag upstairs, Evie," Kylee said, calling Evelyn by her nickname and gesturing the little girl upstairs.

I knew she wanted to talk to me. The reason I was pissed about coming over here in the first place was because I knew this was going to come to a head. She was miserable here, probably 'cause she couldn't get laid. More over, she couldn't find friends to deal with her crap; and now that I had finally moved on, she was trying to punish me. She was still convinced our parents were right.

Since we were little, our parents had this grand idea that we were goin' to end up marryin' each other. I can remember her settin' up little make-believe weddings. Our relationship didn't really grow until college though, when we both went to University of Texas.

I had been fooling around in college. I loved women and sex; there was nothing much more to it than that. I liked the way a woman could make me feel as though I was pleasurin' 'em. I loved makin' them scream my name, calling it out as I pushed harder and deeper. I liked pussy.

My parents, on the other hand, were convinced I needed to be with Kylee. She was desperate. She clung to me and did whatever I needed. If I couldn't find ass that night, she was right there, clothes off, willin' and waitin'.

My parents had this idea that their prodigy son wouldn't be playin' football as a profession. I remember Pops telling me that football was only good for my resume, but that I would take over his precious law firm one day. When I played for University of Texas, my parents were angry and upset because I took football more seriously than school. I was good. I loved hearing the crowd roar and chant my name when I would throw the ball into the end zone. Mom and Pops didn't come to a single game; and when I started barely sliding by in school, they realized I would surmount to nothing. So they'd cut me off. They left their kid for the dust.

I had to make my own way so, thank Heaven, the Houston Texans drafted me that year. I worked my ass off at practice for them, making them feel as though their 1.5 million dollar contract was useful; but Kylee had other plans. Her parents and my parents got together to create this plan to make me take over Pop's law firm. They told Kylee to get off birth control and do what she did with me, which implied fuckin' me.

She had convinced herself that in order to make her parents happy, she had to take drastic means to be with me. So when I was in my first year in the NFL with the Texans, she stopped taking her birth control to get pregnant. One drunken night, when I couldn't find a chick to take home, I crawled into her small, twin-size bed and fucked her blind. When I found out she was pregnant, a brick came down and crashed onto my shit-hole life I was living in. My buddies convinced me my life was ruined. I didn't believe her at first. I thought it was some idea she created in her head to get me to stay with her; but sure enough, the DNA test came back and proved I was the father.

So later on, there I was with a football injury, a pregnant fuck-buddy, and no other direction in life. I married her because I thought maybe that would make Mom and Pops happy. Wrong.

They were miserable with me because I told them that even though my football career was over, I wasn't going back to them. I was never going to work at that godforsaken law firm, and they simply had to accept it. I could remember Pop's saying things like:

"Son, you have a family now; you have to support them, and football won't support them forever." They shunned me from the family when I insisted that I wasn't going to law school.

When I left Houston, because I couldn't handle my parent's disappointment and disapproving glares, Kylee followed me like a lost puppy. I almost felt bad that she had no direction in life. She had no goals, no motivation, absolutely nothin'. I tried making it work with her, but it just couldn't. We slept in separate rooms, only waking up to feed or change the baby. I started sleepin' around again, fuckin' women to get my primal need out. We broke it off, but I vowed to her and to Evelyn that I was a father for life; and just because I wasn't with Kylee anymore, didn't mean that I couldn't be a father to Evelyn.

"Ry," she said, sliding up towards me. I snapped out of my thoughts and looked at her. She was hot; I couldn't deny it. And any other time, I would have taken those hands she was moving along my biceps and thrust them behind her, but I didn't have that need anymore. All I kept thinkin' about was Harper. It wasn't until I met Harper that I realized there was so much more to it. Sex with her was different. I want to wrap her little body around me. I craved her scent and took her all in. I wanted to make love to her every time we were together. When Kylee started to contort her thin body around me, all I could think of was Harper, whose gentle curvature of her boobs and ass sent me into a flurry of excitement.

I snapped out of my thoughts when I heard Kylee's breathing become slow and heavy. I looked up and saw her starin' at me with her version of seductive eyes. She has these deep, black bags under her eyes. Her vulnerability and stress almost made me feel some resemblance of emotion for her. I didn't want to torture her with confusion. It was never meant to be like this, us together. Nothing was supposed to happen this way.

FUCK.

Her face went to meet mine, as she breathed heavily a few inches from me. She was rubbing against me, and my bastard of a dick responded. My cock and my heart aren't always on the same page. I would have taken Kylee right here on the stairs, but Harper isn't just someone. Harper is whom I'm supposed to be with, and I would never do anything to hurt her. She will always be mine. Forever.

"Kylee," I said, pushing her away before this went any further.

"Ry, I don't get it. We are meant to be together. We were married, we have a baby, and our families want us together. I just don't get it; what could go wrong?" she asked in a quiet voice that reeked of desperation.

"A lot went wrong. You want me to be a lawyer…"

"But that is what you are suppose to be! Football clearly didn't work out for you, and now you sit on your..."

"That is enough," I screamed with force.

"I do not want to hear anything else; do you understand, Kylee? I am not with you, and never will be again. I thought you liked Harper? I thought you didn't mind her around Evelyn?" I asked her with genuine curiosity.

"Ry, she doesn't pretend like she is a mom with Evelyn does she?" she finally choked out when she was able to speak.

This caught me off guard. I knew where she was coming from. She felt as though I replaced her with Harper, and now Harper was going to replace her as a mom. I would never let that happen. Harper knew she was always going to be someone important in Evelyn's life, but Kylee would always be her mom.

"I can promise you that will never happen. Evelyn will always see you as Mom. How can she not? You feed her, dress her, and love her more than my own mother even loves me. You are a good mom, Kylee, just not the right person for me."

"I want to go home."

"You are home," I said with force, trying to emphasize that her new base is San Diego, not Houston.

"My parents want me to come home; they want to see Evie. I can go work with my dad as a secretary in his office. My old friends always ask me when I am moving back; I just want to go home."

"No. What about me?" I demanded, trying to keep my voice as steady as I possibly could.

"Come back to Houston. You can go to law school, work for your dad. Come with me," she begged.

"Not an option," I said, knowing I would never leave Harper alone here. And I didn't want to ever face my parents again. In the four years since I left home, I've never once went to face the pieces of shit that birthed me. Why go back when I have everything here?

"I can't stay here; you know I can't," she said in a quiet voice; and without saying much more, Evelyn came bounding down the stairs with her little Barbie princess backpack on.

"Look, Daddy!" she exclaimed, while showing me the front of her backpack with the Barbie's face plastered on the plastic.

"Just like you, hunny," I said, lifting her up and bringing the rest of her stuff outside to the truck.

The conversation between Kylee and me was over…for now. I had to talk to her more about it on Sunday. It would be settled then. Evelyn wouldn't be confronted with two obviously-fighting parents. It was wrong.

Just as I was about to carry her outside and into the car, I heard Kylee shout, "Wait!"

I turned around and saw Kylee running from the inside of the house.

I turned around, with Evelyn still in my arms, and Kylee came up to both of us. She went up on her tiptoes to kiss Evelyn on the forehead, and whispered loud enough in her ears so I could hear.

"I love you, baby," she said and kissed her forehead. I leaned down so she could kiss Evelyn's forehead. She snuck in and pecked me on the cheek.

"I love you, too, and always will. Think about Houston."

I turned around and walked back to my truck, shifting the car seat, making sure it was in right. Kylee would always be a part of my family; and while I loved Harper, I wondered if I was doing the right thing. If Kylee left, I knew my life in San Diego would follow; how hard would Harper be willing to work if I was thousands of miles away?

Chapter 2

Harper

The sun seeped back into the room, and I barely remembered Ryder leaving this morning to go surfing. I spun myself around in his sheets and pressed my toes against the cold wooden floors of his mansion. When I pressed the button to open the shades, the breath in my lungs stopped as I saw the entire ocean cascading into the shore right beneath my feet. It still shook me up that Ryder was not only the owner of this magnificent house, but he was all mine. He owned my every thought, fantasy, and desire I had. He saved me from my past, and from myself. I haven't had one of my nightmares in the month I've been with him, and we haven't spent but a couple nights apart.

I tucked in the sheet over my breast and walked around his room. When Ryder went out surfing, which had been frequently lately, I liked to explore his house and make a nice breakfast that he and Evelyn could come home to.

I ran my hands along his football trophies, which were sitting on the shelf across from his desk. He was so proud of them, just as he was of Evelyn. I grabbed a picture frame, which was next to one of his all-star trophies, and looked at it with a scowl on my face.

It was a moment captured of Kylee and Ryder, with little Evelyn playing on the beach. It looked like it was some sort of professional photo, and was clearly staged. I knew she was always going to be in his life, but it bothered me. I felt as though I had gone through sharing my past with him, and now I have to share his past with the present.

Just as I was studying the frame, I heard a car enter through the carport downstairs. Quickly, I grabbed my sweatpants and a light, racerback tank top over my white bra. I went down the stairs to meet Ryder outside, and saw Evelyn hopping down from the truck.

"Harper!" she screamed, which came out more like hah-puh. She bounded towards me, and I picked her up in a hug.

"Go inside, Evelyn. I was about to start making some breakfast, but I think Daddy can make you pancakes if you ask nicely enough."

"Can we have pancakes, Daddy?"

She ran inside while Ryder came slinking towards me. He had a way about him when he walked; there was a contrast with the gentle ease of how cool he looked, but his slumped shoulders told me he was angry at something that happened. This was usually the case when he'd seen Kylee recently. He would come home distant and irritated.

"What's wrong, baby?" I asked with caution, afraid I would step on his toes. It was something I was used to that bothered Ryder. I was always scared he was going to run away— away to the more logical choice he had. Away to the family he had created years ago. Desperation leaked through my voice, and Ryder immediately snapped his head around.

"Stop actin' crazy woman. There ain't nothing wrong, and you know it. You *know* how much I hate when you question me." He emphasized the "know" and I was struck by the dominance in his voice. Normally, he was loving, and would reassure my anxiety; but this was unlike him. A sting of pain coursed through my bones, and my body pulled away from his. My shoulders slumped down and my heart started beating faster.

"No. I am so sorry." His voice turned back to the compassionate man I remembered. He walked towards me, wrapped his muscular arms ever so lightly around my back, and squeezed me against his strong chest.

"I am just so stressed out with Kylee. She says she wants to move back to Houston."

My jaw must have dropped to the ground. I had no idea she was even considering moving back to Houston. I knew Ryder loved me with all his heart, but he was a parent first. And if he moved to Texas, he would go back to her. He didn't have anything here but me, and I wasn't good enough. I would always be the one on the sidelines supporting him and loving him, but never being good enough. My past taught me not to get too close, so I couldn't even imagine getting close to him.

"I am not going back, just to let you know. So stop thinking about it, Harper. Please," he said, as he graced his velvet and plush lips against mine, sending a wave of electricity pulsing through my body. He wrapped his arms around my waist and lifted me up.

I wrapped my arms around his strong chest and felt each definition of his abs pressed against my breasts. As our kiss deepened, a small moan escaped my mouth, and we were swept into our own world. A sizzle ran through my bones, as I demanded to taste more of his body. He ran his large hands through my hair, tugging slightly through the ends, making my core crave him.

"Ewwww," a little voice squeaked, and I immediately jumped down, hitting my ankle in the wrong place as I landed. I turned around, mortified that Evelyn was standing right there at the door with her hand to her mouth, sticking out her tongue.

"Daddy is kissing Harper. Ew." She thought this was the funniest thing that had ever happened, and started busting out in the cutest giggle I have ever heard. I wasn't sure how to react, but when I heard a hearty laugh, I turned around and saw Ryder laughing hysterically. He had his hands over his abs, clutching on as he crouched over, letting out a wonderful belly-laugh. He ran over to Evelyn and lifted her off the ground, spinning her around a couple times, and throwing her in the air.

"What's so funny, little gal?" She couldn't contain her laughter, and the cute giggle turned into a full belly–laugh, as wonderful as her daddy's.

It was precious moments like this that my worries escaped me and I was brought back to the present, instead of living with my thoughts constantly in the past. A short moment captured, but impacted long into the future. A small smile from a bright, little five-year-old girl could bring happiness to the entire room. I ran up to both of them and pulled them both into a huge bear hug.

"Who is ready for some of Daddy's famous pancakes now?" I asked, looking Ryder right in the deep pools of his blue eyes.

"Me," he said, staring straight at me without hesitation, as if to tell me he is ready for this, for us. He isn't going to Houston without coming up with a solution or some sort of schedule. I could relax…hopefully.

"Let me go get the mail, then I'll be right behind you guys." I always checked the mail because Ryder had a tendency to forget mail ever came. It was such a typical guy thing. I opened the box at the end of the driveway and flipped through a couple bills. One letter struck me as odd because it appeared to be something formal with Ryder's name in calligraphy. Interesting.

When I walked back inside, I could smell the wafting scent of butter.

"I got your mail, babe; it's on the front table. You look like you have some formal invitation or something." I approached him while he stooped down to be on my level, and gave him a small kiss against his cheek.

"It smells delicious in here, doesn't it Evelyn?" I asked the small, female version of Ryder, who was perfectly perched on the table, waiting anxiously for her pancakes.

"Yum!" she exclaimed while rubbing her belly.

When the pancakes were ready, Ryder divided them out and gave us each a couple on a plate. When I looked down, I noticed both Evelyn and I had two heart-shaped pancakes on our plates.

"Heart," she busted out, before diving into her food.

"How sweet," I whispered, before giving him another quick peck on the lips.

"Anything for the most important people in my life." He smiled at me and I felt the butterflies flutter through my stomach. Even though we had been practically living together, the excitement of seeing him show his love for me never fades. I never knew what real love could be like.

I was never loved by my parents, or by Tye, my abusive ex, so I don't know what real love looks like. I am trying to learn everyday what it means to be fully immersed in deep unconditional love, but it's hard. I still have my flaws, like everyone else, but the pain from my past sometimes leaks into my present.

As I started to dive into the buttery goodness of my pancakes, I engaged in conversation with Evelyn about her new daycare friends, her life, and her favorite princess of the week.

"Do you like my daddy?" she asked me out of the blue. Not sure of how to respond, I looked over to Ryder, who doesn't react to the question.

"Of course I like your daddy. He means a lot to me, just like he means to you."

"I love my daddy, so do you love my daddy?" she asked, a very curious five-year–old, indeed.

"I do love your daddy. Is it okay with you if I share him?"

"Yeah, I like you," she said, diving into the last bites of her pancake.

"I love both a'you," Ryder finally said, as he peeped up from his phone. His stare could captivate me, and right now, in this moment, I felt lost in the deep abyss of his eyes. The windows behind him showed the blue ocean that cascaded gently into the shore, which matched the powerful stare of his turquoise eyes. His gaze radiated through my body, gravitating through the deepest parts of my core.

Just as I was about to respond, my phone buzzed, indicating a new text message coming in. It could only be from one person, Skye, my go-to girlfriend, who was busy stressing about her wedding, which was in a year.

S.O.S. Need your help. ASAP. Come to flower shop in dtwn, San Diego.

XOXO

Skye

She was suppose to be picking out the different types of floral arrangements today with her fiancé Jayson, but I assumed that he had to go away on business. He worked with his family at some financial planning company, and frequently had to travel to meet with different clients. The more I got to know him this last month, the more I knew him and Skye were perfect for each other. He grounded her, and loved her for who she was. The bubbly, slightly annoying, but best friend I would ever have. He listened to her when she talked about her family in a serious manner, explaining how she never really had a home with a mom and dad in it; but he also endured her overzealous attitude that, many times, people considered over-the-top.

"Who is it?" Ryder asked, as he saw me checking my phone. He worried I would fall back into old patterns and start being interested in hooking up with other men. His insecurities about keeping me around were annoying at times, but the newfound dominance kept me interested, and kept everything spicy.

"It was just Skye. She has some sort of wedding disaster."

"You need to go to her?" he asked with genuine concern laced in his voice.

"She said she needs me, but I can stay here," I told him, not wanting to ruin his planned-out day with Evelyn. I knew how excited he got when Evelyn is around.

"No, go. Evelyn and I will hang out at the beach today. It's a really nice day out." He got up and grabbed my plate and roughed his hands through my hair.

"Okay, thanks, babe. I'll see you later then." I turned to look at the little girl who was no longer eating her food, but just playing with it. "Evelyn, I am going, but I'll see you later."

"Bye-bye." She waved as I got up to give Ryder a hug in the kitchen.

"I'll miss you," he whispered in my ear in a very low, almost inaudible tone. "Your nipples are peekin' out through your shirt, and I want to wrap my tongue around them, and suck 'em 'til you cry," he moaned oh-so-quietly.

Fuck. He knew exactly what to say when I needed him the most. I craved his touch and his large cock thudding against the walls of my sex. I needed him desperately.

"Mm," was all I could come up with without taking him right there on the kitchen counter. "I'll see you soon," I whispered, and grabbed my bag and headed out to the car.

I couldn't think anymore because if I did, I would be back at the house, begging for more. So I made my way up the beach and towards downtown San Diego, where Skye desperately needed my help picking out flower arrangements.

***

When I got to the flower shop, which was located smack in the middle of the business distract of San Diego, I opened the door and my thoughts immediately switched from Ryder to the pleasant aroma of fresh blossoming flowers. I could hear Skye from the front door, arguing with what I could only assume was the poor owner of this place.

"But you just don't get it; I need those flowers in a light pink, not magenta, but light, almost dusted, pink." I heard her complaining to the older gentleman as I approached.

"Harp! Oh, Harper, I am so glad *you* are here," she emphasized as she crinkled her nose with a pout. "This guy doesn't seem to understand that I cannot have these flowers in a deep pink, but need a light pink."

I gave her a big hug to hopefully ease some of the anxiety she was having about the wedding. Her dad had promised that he would come down for it, and now the whole thing had become such a production. He didn't see Skye very often because he didn't get along with her mother…at all. So, he spent most of his days up in Los Angeles, only giving Skye money when she needed it. Now that he told her he and his new family would attend her wedding next year, she was freaking out over every detail, making sure everything was just absolutely perfect.

"Excuse me," I said politely, looking directly at the poor frustrated salesman, "do you have any of those hybrid roses which are crossed with white and pink? They usually make a very light dusted pink color that I think my friend here wants."

"Ah. Yes. I can get those to you no problem. I wasn't understanding how she wanted us to make the pink, but the hybrid roses I can do," he said, finally understanding what sort of color and flower Skye wanted.

"See, it was that simple." I pointed to her and laughed because I knew the stress she was feeling was finally getting to her; and truthfully, she needed my moral support now more than ever.

"It's not my fault they don't understand." She huffed and gave the guy the rest of her order before we walked out of the shop.

"Now, that took all of thirty seconds; so you dragged me out of spending the day at the ocean to tell you something I could have very well fixed over the phone?"

"But, I needed you," she whined, but we very well knew she really could have fixed all of this if she had just called me.

"Jayson at work again?" I asked.

"Yeah, he had to fly up to San Francisco for some last minute client meeting, but I really needed him here. I just don't know what to do with this wedding," she murmured, clearly stressed out about everything.

"How about we go for coffee or something, and not talk about the infamous wedding that isn't even happening until May?" I asked, pointing to one of those on-every-corner coffee shops across the street.

"Yes, please. I am in definite need of a little pick-me-up," Skye enthused, clicking her heels on the cement pavement beneath her.

Once we sat down and ordered our two vanilla lattes, Skye pulled out her blinged cellphone and texted something to who I could only assume would be Jayson.

"Anything important?" I asked curiously when she didn't look up from her phone.

"Oh, sorry. I am just telling Jay about the floral arrangements. He has some big meeting or something. I don't know, but he isn't answering and I am getting worried," she confessed to me, while running the tips of her manicured hands through her long curled blonde hair.

"Are you worried he is about to bug out on you with this whole wedding?" I asked, knowing that her fears were valid. Her dad left her without a father, and her mother was on her—God only knows which number—, marriage.

"It's just…what if he doesn't want me anymore, in like, ten years. I am not always going to look like this, you know; looks do fade, and I really have nothing else going for me."

"That's bullshit and you know it. Don't talk crap like that, Skye. I am serious. Jayson loves you for who you are, not because you look like you walked off the hottest runway…"

"I do?!" Her ears perked up when I complimented her.

"Shut up. You know what I mean," I said.

"No, I know. I get it. I'm just scared, terrified almost, about what's going to happen. Maybe I really am too young, like you said earlier. Maybe I am rushing into all of this too fast."

"Bullshit," I muffled, irritated she would even begin to think like that.

"You know, when Ryder and I got together, everyone around us kept telling us we were moving too fast into some deep, unknown waters; but they had no right to tell us what they didn't know either. I've never been happier, and couldn't imagine where my life would be right now if it wasn't for him. He is my family, so is Evelyn. I embrace his flaws, his weaknesses, and his life. He is my mind, body, and soul, and I love him more than I could even begin to tell you."

I looked up at Skye, who was shocked at what I said. Ever since I had been with Ryder, I had been trying to open up to people more. Even though it scared the living crap out of me, I wanted Skye to get to know the inner me, and not just the person she brushed on the surface. Together, we had begun exploring our friendship on a deeper level than just what it was externally.

"I know. That's how I feel about Jayson. Like, sure everything was sort of fast, but it just clicked with him. My mom keeps putting these thoughts in my head that he will leave me, or that when he is on his business trips he is cheating on me, so I worry."

"Your mom wouldn't know how to keep a marriage if it depended on her life. What is it now, her fourth? Fifth?"

"Her fourth. I guess you're right…" Skye said, digging into her purse for something. When she pulled out the small black jewelry box, I was immediately alert.

"What's that?"

"It's for you. You don't think I'd be stupid enough to call you down here just because I needed help with the flowers, did you?" She laughed because she knew that's something she totally would do.

"What's this for, though; I don't get it?"

"It's your maid of honor present. I never formally asked you to be my maid of honor, so I am doing it now. Open it up." She said excitedly, pointing to the black box that was now sitting on the table.

I grabbed it from her and pulled the bow she had tied around it. When I opened it, the breath escaped from my mouth. There was a small, delicate necklace, and a charm of my initial with a couple of diamonds on the side.. Under that necklace, there was the exact replica, but instead of an H, it donned an S.

"I know its cheesy and all that stupid shit, but it's my version of friendship bracelets. We both have matching ones," she said, plucking hers from the box.

"I love it. Seriously, Skye, this is too much; but of course, that means it came from you." I got out of my seat and gave her a big bear hug, irritating her because I was messing up her perfect curls.

"Stop it; you're going to make me cry!" She said, as she slipped the necklace around her neck, and I followed her actions with mine. I cannot believe that just a few short months ago, I wanted to run away and leave her behind. She is the sister I never had.

"I'll catch you later," she said, as we both chatted briefly before walking out the door. We turned to part ways towards our separate cars, but not before I heard her perky voice over the loud cars passing through the street.

"Hey, Harper?" She called out as I turned around to face her. "Thank you for always being there for me, no matter what happens." She waved and walked away.

I think I am going to like this new Skye, and this new and improved friendship.

Chapter 3

Ryder

I couldn't get her out of my head the entire day. Fuck. When she left this morning, I could feel her soft tits press up against my chest, and instantly, my dick responded. I tried to cover it up as fast as possible, but I couldn't help that her body demanded to be touched in every which way possible.

I had to shake it off before I faced my daughter; and after she left, I spent the entire day playing on the beach with Evelyn. I almost forgot how fucking amazing Harper looked this morning, when I saw her pulling into the driveway around six.

The thin fabric that separated my eyes from her skin was soaked with sweat. She must have gone to the gym after she saw Skye. She told me that when she saw Kylee kissing me, she started taking up running again to get the frustration out. I understood; it was the reason I surfed.

I don't know if that has been the cure to her nightmares, but she hasn't had one in a really long time. I honestly thought it would be a harder time being with her and watching her wake up and harm herself, but with the running seeming to help, it's been good. But even if she were in the middle of the worst nightmare, I would be her rock.

"Hey, beautiful," I said in the thickest Texan accent I could muster. She said it was "panty-dropping", or some girly shit like that, when I talked with my accent. I didn't hear it, but she even said Evelyn talked with a slight southern accent from being around Kylee and me.

"Don't touch me. I'm all gross." She wrinkled her nose and pretended liked she was smelling her armpits.

"I think you smell amazing. It reminds me of the time…" I said with a hushed tone so Evelyn, who was sitting in the television room, wouldn't hear.

"Stop it." She playfully slapped me and started bringing her gym bag upstairs.

"I am going to grab my stuff and bring it to my place. I have some laundry I have to do, and you're here with Evelyn," she said, before she headed upstairs with me following quickly at her foot.

"What are you talking about?" I asked her with force, frustrated she was just going to run away again. She frequently did this, and it annoyed the crap out of me. Why couldn't she just tell me how she was really feeling? Instead of hitting the nail on the head, she always played this damn game of tag?

"Nothing, just spend time with her," she said, as she started to throw a few sets of her clothes in a bag.

"Damnit, just tell me. What's wrong? You have been here so many times when she is here, so I don't get what's different now?" I asked her, when I finally noticed the diamond necklace draped over her collarbones. "Who is that from?"

"Chill. It's my maid of honor gift from Skye. I don't want to feel like I'm suffocating you," she confessed.

"What are you talking about, woman? We've already talked about this. You aren't a bother to Evelyn or me, so take your clothes back out of the bag. You are staying. Evelyn has to go to bed anyways, and I left you some food from dinner; we went to Max's." Max's was a local grill not too far from me. I never cooked…ever. The few times I have tried have been an epic failure. Poor Evelyn would be raised on chicken nuggets and French fries if it wasn't for her mom.

I walked over to Harper, who was unpacking her clothes from her bag, and kissed her on her head, pulling her tight against my chest.

"Don't ever think you're a burden, okay?" I persisted again.

"Okay," she muffled into my chest.

I walked back downstairs and grabbed Evelyn, who was already falling asleep on the couch. After going through her bedtime routine, the same routine we had been using since she was a newborn, I walked back into the master bedroom, where Harper was typing the start of her novel on the laptop.

I set the monitor on one of the drawers and walked towards her. Her tanned legs were propped in a perfect L-shape on the bed, and all I could think about was ripping them open and tasting the sweetness of her. When I got to the foot of the bed, I crawled up against her.

I rubbed my hands down the upper part of her legs, touching her smooth skin.

"Stop it," she whined jokingly.

"Oh, you want me to stop?" I asked, taking this as a challenge and pushing her computer aside, wrapping her against me, feeling her chest move with each breath.

She started playing with her mouth, biting her lip, and pressing them together, which sent me into another world of needing to feel her. I threaded my hands around the back of her head and pulled her towards my lips. I pushed my mouth, almost violently, into hers, needing to feel her with desperation.

I pulled her shirt up and yanked off her bra to expose her perfectly round tits, and dove onto her nipples to tease her ever so slightly with the flick of my tongue. The escalating moans escaping her mouth turned me hard as a damn rock. My dick was pressed against her, with only the fabric to separate us.

"Fuck," she murmured through groans, and I obliged her by ripping off her shorts and exposing her shaven pussy. Throwing her legs apart, I started kissing her from her tits, down to her navel, trailing my tongue along her skin in between wet kisses as I slowly made my way down.

She arched her back and groaned, demanding more from me; but I just laughed silently, knowing she was building up pressure just to explode at the right time.

When I got down to her soaking wet pussy, all I could think of is putting my rock solid dick inside her and making her cum for hours; but I played this game and ran my tongue around her swollen lips, tasting her sweetness. I licked her thoroughly, flicking my tongue in different directions while placing a finger inside her. Her groans were steady as she let go to the pleasure I was giving her.

"Baby, please," she whimpered.

I moved away from her; she grabbed my pants and took them down, my boxers following.

"Tell me what you want," I demanded, looking at her enormous brown eyes, which were shadowed with seduction. She could just bat her fucking eyelashes to get me to put my dick inside her, but I wasn't about to give up any of my secrets just yet.

"I want you," she barely spoke out, as I moved my lips around hers, teasing her by not pressing them onto hers.

"Tell me what you want," I commanded again, this time a little more forcefully. It was sexy when she dominated.

"I want you…inside of me. Now," she growled, her lips turning into a seductive pout.

At this point, I was so hard it hurt, so I grabbed her hips and slid inside of her, watching her lips form a perfect O as I pushed deeper inside. I grabbed her hips and forced her to ride me on top, throwing her above me, letting her sink onto me as she cried out.

Her hands were on my shoulders as she slammed down on me in a grinding motion, making the pressure inside of me rise, knowing I needed her mouth to taste me, to suck me off. I pulled her off of me, a puzzled look growing on her face. I stood up and stared at her.

"Down." I stared at her. Her mouth gasped, but she obliged willingly, almost excitedly, as she slinked towards my swollen head. She got down on her knees and grabbed me with her fist, shoving me inside of her mouth.

My head tilted back and I succumbed to the pleasure her tongue was giving me.

"Fuck. Yes," I growled at her, letting a few groans escape from my mouth. The repetitive in and out motion of her mouth quickened; with every surmounting push inside, I felt the pressure building deep inside, and immediately knew I needed to release it.

Oh God…yes. I couldn't stand it anymore; her tongue was flicking around, touching the head so lightly, but with just enough pressure. I immediately grabbed her shoulders, desperately wanting to release together, and threw her on the bed. She bounced, but opened her swollen, pink pussy for me.

I shoved inside of her, slamming against her walls repeatedly. Over and over again, she cried out as I pressed firmly against her stomach to push even deeper. I needed to…

"Please, baby," she huffed through panting breaths.

"Say it," I demanded, wanting to hear it from her again.

"I…am…going…to…cum," she managed to squeal out.

I pressed my lips tightly against hers, and kissed her face gently before I released her, and slammed the building pressure of my cock inside of her.

I heard her cries and let go immediately, releasing the pent up frustration, letting the warm fluid sink inside. After one breath of relief, I pulled out, letting the rest of my fluid fall on top of her, before moving to clean myself up. I always loved seeing it; it was my way of marking her as mine.

I grabbed a couple tissues on the nightstand and handed them to her, her face still flushed red with pleasure. I was exhausted and relieved. All I could think about doing now was lying next to her and falling asleep.

When I looked over at the bed, I saw her slight frame curled up in the sheets. I slid into the side I usually slept on and grabbed her by the stomach with one hand. I pulled her against me and started singing a slow lullaby into her hair.

I used to do it with Evelyn, and it would make her fall asleep quicker. It had been working for Harper to make her feel better after her nightmares.

"I love you, Ryder," she said through sleepy yawns.

"I love you so much, Harper. I don't know where I would be without you."

"I'm scared," she whispered faintly.

"I know, baby, I know. But everything will work out." I knew she was referring to our earlier conversation about Kylee wanting to move to Houston. We both knew our fate sat in the hands of Kylee, in the hands of someone who wasn't on our side.

***

Before I knew it, I had to bring Evelyn back to Kylee. Harper had gone to work at Rita's for a little bit, so I decided to meet Kylee at Balboa Park with Evelyn in one of those collapsible strollers.

I saw her immediately, walking towards us down by the long lap-pool. Evelyn and I were playing by the water, looking at the ducks that were hanging out in the small pond structure. I was surprised to see Kylee all done up like she was. She looked like she was goin' out for a night of clubbing. With her thick make up, she looked plain trashy. It's a pet-peeve of mine, huge turn-off.

"Hey, you," she flirted, walking towards me after she gave Evelyn a kiss on the forehead. She looked like a whore trying to swing her hips around to entice me. I applauded her efforts, but all I could think about was the woman I'd have at home, who'd be waiting for me when she got off work.

"Kylee." I was direct in my speech, not faltering even once. She pressed onwards, moving her long fingers around my arms, circling them around my bicep.

"Stop," I demanded.

She huffed and sat down while we watched Evelyn playing fearlessly with the ducks and birds in the park.

"Did you get the invitation from Kayden?" she asked after a few moments of silence.

"What invitation?" I asked.

"Typical. You never change, Ry. Check your mail once in a while, why don't ya?" she drawled. I realized the invitation she's probably talking about was the one Harper had mentioned earlier.

"Are you goin' to tell me what it was about?" I asked.

"Yeah, we are both invited to go to his wedding to Savannah Livingston. He wants us to be in the wedding. Savannah asked if I could be in her bridal party, and I guess Kayden wants to have you as a groomsman."

"Oh, yea. Damn, I miss Kayden."

Kayden Knox and I grew up together in Texas. We both played football together at University of Texas; but when I left for the NFL, Kayden took my place. We both loved to go out and party, always hanging out at his clubs and picking up chicks, but I left Texas before I got to meet Savannah. From what I hear, he is completely pussy-whipped.

Savannah knew Kylee from some function they attended at their country club and they were friends. I guess they want us to come to Texas to their wedding. I would be all over hanging out with the old bros, I haven't been back to Houston, or Texas for that matter, since I left; I just didn't want to deal with family crap.

"Are you going?" she asked.

"I'll have to see if I can get off work. I don't know. I haven't been back since I left."

She looked down before she spoke, "I know, but I was thinking maybe I could just see if I like it there. If maybe we'd like it there…together?"

"What?" I asked, confused.

"I mean…we could see if it would be an option if I could move back there. I want to talk to my parents, and maybe even yours…"

"No way. You can talk to them all you want, but no way am I going to see them. No fucking way, Kylee."

"Ry, I think you should at least hear them out. My mom told me your's has been asking about you. Just hear 'em out."

"Nope. No way, no how. Not happenin'. I'll call Knox. Tell him I'm comin' to the wedding but I ain't going to Houston."

"Okay, Ryder. Well, I am going to Houston before the wedding. Evelyn is going to be the flower girl, so she is coming with me."

"Fine. Where are y'all staying, at Knox's place? The one in Galveston?"

"No, the one in Sugar Land. Savannah said I could stay in one of the rooms. That place is huge. She said you could, too…"

"We are staying in different rooms."

I was trying to figure out how I was going to tell Harper; she was going to flip out.

"I know, Ry, I know," she said looking away, clearly annoyed that I kept turning her down.

"I'll call Knox; we'll figure this out."

After a few quiet moments, Kylee asked in her genuine voice, and not that fake bullshit she puts on to entice people, "Is Harper going?"

"I've got to see if she can. She's starting school back up again, so I don't know. Honestly, I don't know if I want her there. It'd be too tough, being in the same state as everything that happened with my parents. I don't want them to pull something and have her there to witness it."

I saw a glimpse of evil in Kylee when I told her I didn't want Harper to come, but all she could do was click her tongue and say, "How close can you get to someone without showing them all the different sides of you?"

She walked over to Evelyn, picked her up, and both of them said goodbye.

"See you in Texas."

It was August and the sun was blazing down, sweat was glistening off my arms as my shirt clung tightly against my chest.

Fuck. If I was going to go to Texas, I had to call Knox. I punched his number into my phone. He hashed out all the details of his big day, sounding really exciting when he talked about Savannah. In the back of my mind, I had to wonder if that's what I sounded like when I talked about Harper.

He told me I would be stayin' on his side of the house, and that he had an extra room for me, which saved me from Kylee's crap. I didn't want her tryin' anything and messing anything up with what I had now.

I asked him if Harper could come, but he hesitated. He had assumed that Kylee and I were still married, and I didn't have a plus one because she was already invited. I told him it wasn't a big deal and that Harper was probably not even goin' to make it. We hung up and I went to the bar, where I was meeting up with Finn, Skye, and Harper.

***

When I got to the bar, after bein' stuck in rush hour traffic, I saw Finn sitting in a corner table, drinkin' a pale ale. Harper and Skye weren't going to meet us for another hour, so I grabbed a beer over at the bar before headin' to the table.

"What's up, brah?" Finn asked in his stereotypical SoCal accent.

"Nothin', just got off the phone with Kayden. You know him and Savannah are getting married?" I asked. Finn had knew about Knox by me talking about him.

"No way, dude. Totally rad. You going?"

"Yeah, thinking about it. The weirdest part was that he thought me and Kylee were still together, so I didn't really get a plus one; don't know what to do."

"Doesn't Harper have school starting up anyways? She'll be fine. You're going to go support your buddy is all. Right?"

"Yeah, I guess your right; I just don't know how I am going to tell her. She is going to think I am abandoning her, or that I don't want her there, or something."

"Just tell her after you give her some of that D, dude." Finn joked, laughing hysterically.

We talked about the surfing competition he kept wanting me to enter in October. When I heard two heels clinking, I turned around and immediately spotted Skye coming towards us. She was a sweet girl, troubled like Harper, but maybe that's why they got along. She never fit in, though; I never understood why Harper liked her, because she exuded wealth, something I wasn't a huge fan of. Harper came in behind her in her comfortable and more sensible flip flops. Finn cleared his throat beside me. He loved to flirt, period. He especially loved flirting with hot girls, like Skye.

"Hey Ry," Skype called out, coming over and air-kissing me on the cheek. "Finn."

"Thank God someone with taste is here," he joked, and gave her a kiss on the cheek. Really, it was Harper who commanded my attention. She was stunning with her hair pulled back in a ponytail and dressed in little clothing since it was so hot outside. What she had on made me want to rip it off and take her in the crowded bar.

"Hey, baby," she murmured, before kissing me softly on the lips. They both sat down next to us, and Skye ordered the typical mojito, and Harper a summer beer.

"Your boy here has got to enter this competition. Convince him," Finn said to Harper.

"Competition?"

"Yeah, I told you about it; the one in October. Finn wants me to enter. Pat thinks it's a good idea for my image or somethin'," I responded.

"You should do it. Why not?" Harper asked.

"Yeah! I would know a famous surfer!" Skye chimed in.

"Hey now ladies…" Finn interjected.

"I said I would think about it."

"I think it's a really good idea, baby," she said, before leaning closer into my ear and cupping it with her hands so that no one could hear. "Seeing you ride those waves is such a turn on."

God damn that woman was sexy. She knew how to press every button to turn me on. Fuck, she really was beautiful in that hey-sexy-come-hither sort of way.

"Skye, how is the wedding coming along? Thinking anymore of dumping that rich fiancé of yours and hanging out with a pro-surfer all day?" Finn joked.

"You wish, Finn!" She laughed at him and then turned to order another one of those fancy drinks.

We all enjoyed ourselves laughin' about different people who walked in, or just life in general. Finn was drunk…like verging on the line of belligerently drunk. We had been there for a couple hours, and as per Skye's request, we had done a couple of shots in between our beers.

"Finn," Skye cried in her obnoxious voice that got really high at the end of her sentences.

"Skye. Oh, my beautiful, unattainable Skye. What could you possibly want?" Finn slurred out.

"Tell us something that no one else knows. I want to know a secret," she said conspiratorially.

"Lets not go there, Skye," I interjected, lookin' over at Finn, hopin' he wouldn't say anything and keep his fuckin' mouth shut about everything. Harper was just sitting in the corner, enjoyin' the scene that was unfolding, completely unaware that Finn just heard something I wasn't prepared to tell her yet.

"Oh, I got a good story; you ladies ready to hear this?" Finn asked, completely oblivious to my glares.

"Yeah, baby!" Skye shrilled.

"Tell us, Finn," Harper spoke up.

I swear to God, if this asshole said anything, I'd kill him. Literally, pound his mother fuckin' face into the ground.

"There is this guy I know. A total fucking hottie for you ladies..."

Harper and Skye both laughed, but I continued starin' him down, deadpan in the eyes. This fucker...

"Anyways, he was this massive playboy when I first met him, just loved fucking those ladies sideways until they fell down and begged him to stay for more."

"Ohhh my," Harper squealed, but clearly interested in knowing more of the story.

"He has this kid too, with this chick who is the hottest of them all. No one knows why he won't just fuck her senseless and continue doing it, because she is truly a walking goddess. That's beside the point. The point is now, he is going to take both women for a spin. He is bringing the one, his ex, back home...home, where he..."

My eyes were frozen in place. I knew I needed to move to attack this son of a bitch, and beat the shit outta him, but Harper was just staring at him breathlessly. Skye's bubbly domeanor was immediately taken over by someone who sat there with a sullen look. Finn's drunk ass had absolutely no idea what he was doing, and he kept gesturing around and drinking his beer while telling his story.

"He got invited to this guy's wedding, and he is going to the wedding with— get this—his ex-wife." He started laughing hysterically, but Harper looked at me with sadness in her eyes. She looked the way I saw her before she met me: broken and confused. Skye slapped Finn across the face.

"Shut the fuck up, you asshole," she said seriously, breaking the silence that echoed in the loud bar.

"I can't..." Harper turned to me, looking at me with her nose wrinkled in disgust, "I just cant..."

She got up from her seat and walked out, with Skye in tow.

"Why the fuck did you say that shit? I am goin' to kill you, Finn, seriously."

"I totally thought you had already told her. I swear. I don't know," he said truthfully, chugging his beer.

"Call me tomorrow, take a cab." I chucked him a couple of twenties and walked out to try to find Harper. I hoped she wasn't already gone.

Chapter 4

Harper

I cannot even begin to fathom why that asshole would start telling that story.

"I am so sorry, Harp. When I told him to tell us something we don't know about him, I didn't know that is what he was going to say. I am sorry," Skye said, trying desperately to keep up with me in her pumps.

"It's not your fault. I'm going home. Call me tomorrow."

"Are you okay? You can come stay with me."

I turned around to face her, and stared at her with an empty look on my face. I was disgusted by that piece of shit. I couldn't even describe my anger with him. I wanted nothing to do with him anymore. I wanted to run away from here; he would just be added to my list of big disappointments.

I knew all of this was too good to be true. Ryder was going back to Kylee, going back to Texas, and probably would stay there for good.

"I'm fine. Call me later," I said, leaving Skye there and turning the corner. I walked a couple of blocks down, hoping the fresh air would calm me; I felt nothing but the numb feeling of bleakness.

I turned around to see if by any stroke of luck Ryder was following me, or if he wanted to chase after me, but I didn't see anything but a cloak of darkness.

I looked down at my phone and saw the text messages that kept coming in. They were coming from Skye and Ryder, and I didn't have the courage, or the strength, to open them.

I didn't what to deal with any of this. Why was it always so complicated to fall in love?

I walked until my legs were going to give out on me, and realized I was in front of a small dive bar. I walked in and took a seat on the old, rugged, leather barstool. It was dimly lit and full, mostly with older men in leather jackets and jeans.

"What can I getcha?" the bartender mumbled, clearly miserable with his shitty job.

"Corona, please," I replied, and pulled my purse tightly against my chest.

When the beer arrived, I sat and watched the small television playing the baseball game in the corner. I felt the stool next to me shift, and could see a large figure in the corner of my eye.

"You here alone?" I turned around and saw a guy with blonde hair, who had a couple wrinkles on his face.

"Yup. Alone," I emphasized, looking back at the game and sipping my beer.

"You watch baseball?"

"Nope." I tried to turn away again, but the guy wasn't feeling it.

Honestly, I had no idea what I was doing. I wanted to be alone for a while, sit with my thoughts and figure out why Ryder would even think about going to Texas without telling me. Why couldn't I go with him as a date to the wedding? How could he imagine going to Texas for the first time in years, and not bring me? It was all illogical. A wall he set that I was desperately trying to climb but couldn't, and kept falling down. Over and over again…

"What's your name?" the strange guy next to me asked.

I turned around to him and figured, why not? If Ryder could do it to me, why not move on the way I knew how?

"Harper, what's yours?" I slid my seat closer to his.

There were thoughts running through my mind, telling me I was making the wrong decision; but knowing this was the only way to cope, I tried to fix the feelings I was drowning in.

"Sam. You lookin' to drink another one of those?" he asked, pointing at my already half-downed beer.

"Sure. Why not, right?"

"That's the spirit." He pointed and motioned to the bartender for a refill on the beer I was drinking.

Fuck him for doing this for me. I was doing this because of Ryder. I was doing this because he knew how sensitive I was, and now he was taking his ex-wife as a date to a wedding.

"So, you single?" I asked, winking at him.

Seriously, who lets their drunken best friend blurt that out at a bar? How can you be that insensitive of an asshole, not to pull your girlfriend, who you practically live with, aside and tell her?

I was going to lie to this guy and live my life as a different person, even if it was just for tonight. I needed to be someone else for tonight. I needed to be the old Harper, the one who would fuck anything blind.

"I am. Are you?"

I thought about this. Was I single? What didthis even mean for us? I can't even begin to explain how I felt, or fathom how I *should've* felt right then. I wanted to feel angry, bitter, or sad, but I felt numb to the world. It's my go-to emotion: numbness. It takes the pain and suffering from my world and transported it somewhere else. Fuck this. Seriously. I can't do this anymore. I couldn't be with someone who doesn't make me a priority. I had been there and done that. Never again will I be someone's number two when I deserve to be number one.

"It's complicated," I answered, while drinking the beer the bartender had just poured.

Where do I go from here? Do I run away like I am used to doing, and fall back into my old habits of sleeping with random men, like I was trying to do right then? Do I go home, or go back to his place? I didn't know what to do. I simply had no idea where to go from here. I'm lost, alone, and sick and tired of feeling like this all the time. When would it be my turn to be in love, and life be a little easier? When would it ever be my turn to feel like someone in my life is there to make me happy, and not just to turn around on me? Who could answer these questions for me?

"You ever been in love?" I asked randomly, taking him off guard, knowing never to hit on a guy by talking about love or their exes; but this was different.

I needed to know if all men acted like Ryder. Ryder was always supposed to be there for me…always. Now he was going back to Texas, and who knows if he even considered asking me. This wouldn't be a big deal if one, he wasn't taking his ex-wife as a date to a wedding, and two, if he wasn't going to a place that was emotionally devastating for him. Ryder hadn't been back to Texas in years because he hated his family and what they did to him, shunning him because he didn't believe in what they wanted.

"Love? No. Not in love; don't plan on falling in love. You into that kinda shit?" the stranger next to me asked.

I pondered the question for a second. Could I ever open up to trust Ryder again after all this? Everything for us was intense and fast. We fell in love too quickly, and we fight at the drop of a hat. It was as if the world was trying to force us together while pulling us apart. We needed each other because of this unexplainable emotion we contained, but at the same time, no one around us knew what to do. Kylee was jealous, his parents probably hated me because I wasn't Kylee, and Finn was a stupid drunk. How can you be with someone when everyone works so hard to keep you apart? Maybe it's just not worth it anymore….

"Yes, I do believe in falling in love," I said, after waiting a couple seconds to think about it.

Of course I wanted love. A couple months ago, I would never admit to this kind of thing. I would never confess I wanted to be in love with someone; but now, everything was different. With Ryder, I felt the world around me. I felt what happiness and joy was like. I felt what it meant to be full and complete, but that meant I could also feel sorrow, anger, and betrayal. Like right then, I felt betrayed by him.

"You wanna go someplace a little more quiet?" the stranger asked.

Did I? Did I want to go home with him and do all this all over again? What would Skye think? More importantly, what would I think about myself again? I would be that Harper I vowed never to be, and here I was doing the same thing again.

No, I don't think I wanted to go home with him; I wanted to go see Ryder. I'd like to give him one chance to make me believe him but if he couldn't, I was done. That was it for me. Everyone deserved a second chance, I believe that fully, but sometimes second chances lead to third and fourth and I don't want that. So one more chance for Ryder. I would at least give him thatGive him the chance to at least explain what Finn meant, or what he was going to be doing with Kylee and Houston. Ryder made me feel, period. He allowed me to experience what emotions were, and sometimes that meant feeling a loss like this. But that low feeling was countered by an unexplainable emotional high. I needed him as much as I knew, deep in my heart, he needed me.

"Sorry, I don't think so. Thanks for the beer," I said, and walked out, priding myself on how I didn't go home with him. I walked out with my head held high.

I was still that independent Harper everyone knew, but this time, I had the support of a man who loved me. When I got outside, I hailed a cab, and drove straight to Ryder's house.

***

I pulled up to the expansive beach mansion and quickly paid the cab driver. I was fumbling for my key in my purse while standing on the front step when I heard the door rush open.

"Harper," Ryder said breathlessly, the lines in his forehead etched deep into his skin. He was stressed, and the redness of his eyes showed his worry and exhaustion.

"We need to talk," I said, pushing past him and walking towards the kitchen to get a glass of water.

"I know; I should have told you earlier. I am so sorry," He pronounced, helping me get the water from the filtered jug.

"I don't get why Finn had to tell me when he was drunk. I don't even know what's going on. Tell me," I demanded.

"I got invited to an old friend from Texas's wedding, Kayden Knox. His fiancé, Savannah, also knew Kylee. They figured we were still married and would come as dates, and asked if we would be in their wedding party. When I called Knox, he said he figured since we were married and already invited, we didn't need plus ones. I told him that Kylee and I had divorced, and I was seein' you."

"Okay, so did you get the plus one?" I interjected.

"Not exactly. Something about there not being enough plates; but I thought it would be okay with you because it was right around when school would start, and I knew how busy you said you were goin' to be. I just figured…"

"I know what you figured, Ryder, but you can't just not ask me. Even if I was going to say no, don't you think it's important to ask me if I wanted to come? I mean, you are going to Texas for the first time in four years. I would invite you if I ever went back to Chicago, just for moral support."

"I get it. You have every right to be mad at me, and you have no idea how bad I want you there with me. I was goin' to tell you, I swear to you, I was; I just didn't get the chance to before we met up with Finn. I didn't want our night to be completely ruined."

"But it was anyways. Don't you see that? It was ruined because this got out and I had to hear it from Finn and not from you," I said, watching him from across the kitchen. He didn't get close to me; instead, he stood by the sink, running his hands through his hair repeatedly.

"Yeah, I do. Please, Harper. Please, forgive me. I don't know what I would do without you. Why does it always seem like there is something keepin' us apart? I need you in my life, and I don't know where I would be without you here."

I thought about what he said, and truthfully, I felt the same way. I needed him with me every second of every day, but I also knew his other responsibilities. If an old friend wanted him to stand up in his wedding, I shouldn't be the one to stop him. I had to trust Ryder wasn't going to be like my abusive ex, Tye. I had to trust that Ryder wouldn't betray me and leave me for the next best thing.

I could see tears welling up in Ryder's eyes and moved over towards him. When I got close enough, he opened his arms wide, and I ran towards them. These were the arms I felt safe in. These were the arms that comforted me in my darkest times, and carried me through the happiest. It's so hard to fall in love, but when it's right, you know, because everything seems to just click.

"When is this wedding, anyways?" I asked curiously when we parted briefly.

"It's in late August, so pretty soon. I would fly out on a Thursday and be back on a Sunday. I want you to come with me. I don't care what Knox says, I'm sure he will be fine with it. The asshole is rich enough; he can afford another plate. Plus, he owes me a couple favors."

"No, I want you to go. You should be able to go to a wedding without me, especially if you're a groomsman. I'm just scared with Kylee there. I mean, what if she convinces you to stay."

"She wouldn't. I would never factor her opinion into that conversation without gettin' you involved too. We would have to come up with a solution and then talk to her. You come first Harper, always and forever."

"Are you guys staying at the same place?" I asked, really hoping that Ryder wasn't going to be staying anywhere near Kylee.

"We are both stayin' at Knox's place, but it's huge. He has somethin' like 30 rooms in the entire house, so I won't even see her unless it involves Evelyn. I promise you, I won't go near her."

"Are you going to visit your parents?" I asked hesitantly, knowing that talking about his parents always caused friction. Instead, I glanced over at him, and he appeared to be calm. He was listening to me and answering all the questions I had. I think he wanted to ease any worry I had.

"No. Kylee is going to Houston with Evelyn to visit her parents, but we already discussed that I will not be goin' anywhere near them. Kayden's mansion is in Sugar Land, which is a city on the outer limits of Houston. I am not ready to see my parents. They didn't care about their son, and haven't called me in almost four years, so why should I reach out and contact them?"

"I know it's hard, baby," I said, reaching up to stroke his cheek.

"Will you please forgive me? I know I suck, but I need you here with me." He gestured at his house.

"I need you to promise you'll talk to me first before you go tell your friends, especially when its something serious like going back to Texas for the first time in four years. Okay?"

"I am so sorry; I really shouldn't have. Yes, of course. Next time, I will tell you immediately after somethin' happens, but now, I need you," he said with aggression and gentleness at the same time.

He pulled me deep into his chest, and I could smell the sweetness of vanilla and mint. I breathed him in heavily, and felt his arms tighten their grip.

"I love you so much, Harper," he muffled into my hair, while kissing the outer lobe of my ear ever so slightly.

"I love you, too. I am going to miss you when you are gone," I said truthfully.

"You have no idea how bad I am goin' to miss you, but the invitation is open. If you want to come, I will make it happen."

"I want you to make me feel better," I whispered in his ear, insinuating that I needed him inside of me. I wanted him exploring my body and showing me what I meant to him. I wanted him to run his fingers through every nook and cranny my body had to offer. I needed him to make love to me…now.

His fingers pushed through my hair, pulling back slightly, and his lips came across my neck. He started kissing me, easing down my neck with his lips pressingly lightly. When he got to the middle of my neck, he started sucking on my tender skin, while letting out slight groans between ragged breaths. Gently, he nibbled the skin on my neck, and dug his teeth in just enough to cause a flutter down in the deepest parts of my sex.

His kisses didn't stop, but all the while, he moved his hands towards the hem of my shirt and pushed up, exposing my navel. My black lace bra was exposed and he moved his mouth down towards my breasts. He took his time, gently easing his way down. While pushing aside the cup of my bra, he exposed my flushed skin and he grabbed my nipple with his teeth, pulling up on it, sending a burst of painful pleasure throughout my body.

His hands went behind my back, and slowly, he took off my bra with one swift movement of one hand. My breasts spilled out and his tongue continued circling my nipple while his hand explored the other. He took his time, caressing me with gentle ease and hungry moans.

When he was finished, he moved slowly down my navel, kissing me on the way down, and letting his tongue drag until I felt a need claw from the inner-most part of my body. A need to feel him inside of me, but instead of obliging, he was teasing me, making me want more from him. His mouth moved gently, and when he got down to my center, he licked around carefully, but quickly unbuttoned his pants and let his boxers drop with a thud on the floor.

Every time I saw him without clothes on, I was mesmerized by the beautiful, masculine creature that stood in front of me. His abs looked almost drawn on they were so perfectly formed, and when he sucked his breathe in, they flexed naturally. His black hair was slicked back and longer now, which contrasted violently with his ice blue eyes and his crisp features. His jawbones were perfectly chiseled; they emphasized a contoured look most makeup artists would die to recreate. The slight shadow on his face created a stubbly look that tickled me when he ran his face over my bare skin, but was so completely sexy. When I would look at him, I wondered how I got so freaking lucky to be with a sex god like him.

"You look so hot like that, Harper. I want you like this all the time," he commanded while staring at me.

He grabbed the button of my shorts with his mouth and with a quick movement, he pulled with his teeth, and my jeans unbuttoned. He quickly removed them and added them to the pile already on the floor. His hands moved towards my underwear, and in one swift move, they were ripped in two and fell on the floor.

"I'm going to have no underwear left to wear if you keep doing that," I huffed, but secretly thinking it was the hottest move he could ever do.

"I'll buy you more." He oozed with sexual desire and determination as he moved towards me. We were now on the floor of the kitchen, but he grabbed me and threw me over his shoulder with my ass up in the air.

"Hey, what the…" I shouted as he opened the patio door.

We were standing on the balcony now, and I could hear the waves roaring onto the shore below us. It was pitch black, and the only light that illuminated was the one coming from the living room. I couldn't see anything, but I could feel him grabbing my waist. He pressed me hard against the balcony, which was only wide enough for my ass. He propped me up and growled as he pressed his throbbing erection against the top of my thigh. The slightest touch of him sent a cold shiver spiraling through my spine.

Just as the cold ocean wind was blowing against us, he gripped tightly and shoved inside of me with such force, I screamed out in pleasure.

"Hold on," he commanded, as he thrust his rock-hard cock inside of me with such vigor, I thought the balcony was going to break from underneath me.

I arched my back and let my hair flow in the wind as he pounded into me over and over again. I couldn't contain myself, so I howled out loud with great force and pleasure. I was definitely a screamer tonight.

He grabbed me from off the balcony, and while he stood with his back against it, he carefully bounced me up and down his large cock, making me moan as he dropped me down, and pant as he pulled me up.

"Fuck, Harper, you are so goddamn wet," he cried out, collapsing against the cold, wooden balcony.

He mounted me, and I could feel the cold wood of the balcony at my back. I took in the ocean waves as they crashed to shore. I was taken back to the first time we made love on the beach, and suddenly, this moment became much more emotional. I needed to feel him inside of me, and without having to say it, Ryder understood. He slowly and repetitively moved every inch of his cock in, then out of me. He tooks his hands and gripped my shoulders as he explored the deep part of my pussy with his cock.

He stared at me with his brilliantly blue eyes; they sparkled, even in the darkness. I observed each work of art on his body, gently touching the tattoo on his shoulder with the tips of my fingers. I took my time exploring each nook and cranny of his body. I took my time; in this moment, Ryder was the only thing that mattered in the world.

He was now watching himself glide in and out of me. Ryder arched his back and put his hands to his ass as he pushed inside of me at a quicker pace. Almost unsure of what he would do with his hands, they found their way to my backside, while he pulled our torsos closer, causing our chests to touch as our bodies engaged in a duet of movement. His fingertips found their way to my breasts and pulled on them lightly, the pressure causing me to groan with pleasure.

His cock was throbbing inside of me, and the continuous movements had me crying out. I needed him to thrust faster and deeper inside of me.

"More. Faster, deeper," I managed to squeak, and he obliged and put more pressure on my clit. Every time he thrust inside of me, I could feel his fingertip massaging my clit with pleasure. He was fueling my desire, and I was on the brink of releasing.

"I want to feel you cum inside of me, baby," I called out.

This got him excited again, and he picked me up from the ground and hastily dropped down on the patio recliner with me on top. I bounced up and down quickly, shoving his large cock deep inside me. Ryder grabbed my hips, guiding me up and down, over and over.

"Fuck. Fuckkkkk!" He moaned.

"Make me....cum," I screamed after him, needing him to release the built up pressure inside of me.

He grabbed me again, and pushed me back to the balcony railing. Quickly, Ryder spun me around, and I braced my hands on the railing, prepared to take this pounding from him as he entered me from behind. I stood on my tiptoes as he thrust his enormous cock deep inside of me. I needed this release, now!

"Cum with me, baby," he moaned between thrusts.

"I can't...hold...it," I cried, as he pounded into me over and over again, each time getting deeper and deeper.

"No. Not yet," he demanded, shoving into me so quickly that my hands were slipping off the railing and I couldn't hold it any longer.

"I need...to..."

Holy shit. I couldn't stand it anymore. The built up pressure was growing and I needed to explode all over his warm cock. My pussy was swollen with pleasure, and his erection was still thrusting deep inside of me. My stomach was now slamming against the railing of the balcony as his grunted.

"Now," he commanded with force, not faltering.

I let go, crying out with immense pleasure, and felt a release escape from my core. I felt a rush of warm liquid all over me, and we came together. As our orgasms ripped together, we both cried out towards the vast ocean.

"Yes, baby. Yes," Ryder breathed.

He pulled out of me and I felt my knees buckle as I collapsed on the nearest recliner. He didn't say much, but walked back into the house. I closed my eyes and let the night breeze glide over me as I steadied my breath.

When I heard the patio door slide back open, I saw him there, with his cock at half-mast, carrying two glasses of ice-cold water. How did I get so lucky to be with someone like him? He was sensitive enough to understand my needs without even needing direction.

I couldn't believe I had ever thought about being with another person, because no one could compare to the amazing moments we shared together. I needed him in my life, forever embedded in my core.

He slipped into the same tight chair and gave me my water. We both sat smashed together, watching the stars above us tinkle in the night sky. It felt like hours that passed us by, just sitting there in silence.

"Please don't ever scare me like that again," he whispered, sounding like a small child.

"Me? Scare you? You scared me, Ryder; you still do."

"I know, baby; but you have to learn to trust me. I love Kylee, but not like that. I love her because she is the mother of my daughter. I love you, but you scare me. I am scared you're going to slip through my fingers."

"I would never. I don't know where I would be if you weren't here today. Plus, the sex…is just too good to give up now." I smiled, and he shook his head and laughed at me.

"You do have the best pussy." He looked over at me and we both busted up laughing.

"I love you, sweets," he said, kissing me gently on the lips. "Oh, I have an idea." He jumped up and walked back inside.

When he came back, he had his hands full of pillows. He pulled a couple of the recliners together to make an L-shaped sofa and told me to come over.

He added the comfiest cushions to the recliners, and we both slipped on our underwear before laying on the makeshift couch.

He held me tightly against his chest, seeing as there wasn't much room on the couch, and he put the blanket over us.

"Goodnight," he whispered in my ear. I turned over to face him, my chest pressed tightly against his. I had never slept outside, just mere feet above the beach. It was invigorating. I had done so much more in my time with Ryder than I had done with anyone else, and I wanted to keep exploring.

I wasn't done writing our romance.

Chapter 5

Ryder

I got onto the plane and put my bag up in the overhead compartment above the first-class seat I had upgraded at the counter. I flashed my credit card and flexed my arms to the kind flight attendant at the desk, and boom, upgrade sealed. I was one of the last on the plane because I had debated on whether or not I should leave. I'd been having flashbacks of this morning with her, as she showed me the ins and outs of her body. I wanted to show her I loved her over and over again. When she finally convinced me to go, I remembered the pain on her face as I walked into the airport. Dropping my smile, I realized I missed her. I was scared and alone. I sounded like a dumbass for admittin' that, but I needed her here with me. I realized that Harper needed to go on with her daily routine. I couldn't be that obsessive, overprotective prick. I promised that I'd call her once I landed at Hobby Airport in Houston.

In a few short hours, I would be back "home", or rather the place I called home growing up. I arranged for a car to pick me up from HOU airport to take me directly to Sugar Land without stoppin'. Kylee took Evelyn to Houston a couple days ago to visit, but the less time I could spend there, the better. I wasn't about to give Pops the chance to weigh me down with questions about the goddamn law firm.

The plane took off, so I put on my headphones and listened to some Dustin Lynch.

***

When we landed, I grabbed my bag, and walked right to the waiting town car. I needed a Bud and quick. The driver took us down the highway; the same one I used to take to the Reliant Stadium. Instantly, I was antsy. My knees started bouncin', and my fingers tappin'. This damn weekend couldn't end soon enough.

After an hour, the driver pulled up to Knox's mansion. Damn, he did so well in life that I almost envied him. He came out of the house with two beers in his hand

"Christ, dude. Thank God you remembered," I said, giving him a pat on the back and grabbing the rest of my stuff from the driver.

"I'm just glad you're here. I see you lost a bit of your accent," Knox joked.

"Yeah, a little; but I didn't lose my taste for a good ole' Bud."

Knox laughed. When we got inside of his house, he led me to the left wing.

"Got your stuff in there, let me know if you need anything. Meet us outside when you're done. Savannah's here and she wants to meet ya," he said.

I dropped my stuff down on the bed and pulled out my suit, throwing it over the chair. I studied the bed and it dawned on me I was going to have to spend the entire weekend without Harper. One of the only times we wouldn't be spending the night together since we started bein' official and all. I was goin' to have the worst case of blue balls I've ever had.

I grabbed my phone and gave her a call.

"Hey, baby. I miss you and you just left," she said when she picked up. She was a recipe for an instant hard-on.

"Damn, I miss you. Reconsider coming, please? I can get you on the first plane here, you can be here tonight. The wedding isn't even until Saturday."

"You know I can't; I have school and want to spend time helping Skye. It's okay," she murmured into the phone.

"I need you," I growled, imagining her sweet ass in the bed right in front of me.

"Me too, baby; me too," she said into the phone in her sweet husky voice. Not only was it going to be hard being in this ghost town, but having her away from me was harder.

We talked for a while; then, when I finished my beer and needed another one, we hung up the phone, promising to talk later. I walked outside where I could see Knox and a couple others hanging by the pool.

I heard the country music pumping and opened the door, only to be welcomed by a cooler of every beer ever made. I picked up another one before heading over to the group.

"Yo, Knox," I hollered.

"Ryder, come here. I want you to meet Savannah."

He gestured to the pretty blonde in the corner. She reminded me of Kylee and I could see why they were friends. They hung out in the same sort of circles.

"Pleasure to meet you, ma'am," I spoke in my southern accent, using 'sir' and 'ma'am' was a sign of respect down here. It always confused the hell outta me when I got rude remarks when I said them in California.

"It's nice to meet you, Ryder. I have heard a lot about you. This is my friend Brooklyn, and the rest of the gang."

I waved to the group, and finished with introductions.

"When's Kylee comin'?" I asked Savannah.

"She said she is coming with Evelyn tonight after dinner. I must apologize, Ryder. No one knew y'all even got a divorce."

"It's all good." I looked over at Knox, who immediately changed the subject.

"Kylee said her parents are going to watch Evelyn here tonight while we go to my club. You in for old time's sake?" he asked me, not wanting Savannah to press on the divorce issue.

"I'm down." I needed to get drunk tonight with my buddy, who was about to be a married man.

"Congrats, again, you two," I said, before water-falling the rest of my beer and grabbing another one.

We hung out for a couple hours on the porch, and by the time Kylee came, I was already buzzed.

"Hey, babe," she said, coming over to Savannah and kissing her on the cheek. She was clearly in her element. She looked more relaxed and wasn't desperately clinging to me for attention.

"Where's Evelyn?" I interrupted, pissed she was acting all stupid. She couldn't be comfortable here. Nope. No fuckin' way! I didn't want her thinkin' 'bout moving back to this hellhole.

"She's upstairs with my mom. She's staying here watching her for tonight. Hello to you too, Ryder."

I shrugged her off and went upstairs to change, and to say hello to my daughter.

After dinner, we all got together and took one of Knox's stretched limos to the club. While everyone started mingling, I immediately went over to the bar to grab another drink. The buzz from earlier was starting to wear off and it was pissing me off. I missed my girl, who was stuck at home because of some self-centered little bitch here,and the fact I was back in Texas wasn't a good combo.

"Slow down, buddy," Knox said, coming over to me.

"I'm good dude, no worries."

"Tell me about this Harper girl," he asked, while grabbing a couple beers for us and walking towards his VIP section.

"I love her, man. I know I sound like such a pussy, but she has been the best thing to ever happen to me. Kylee and I just never clicked. It was fucked up from the start."

"She should have come; I would have loved to meet her. If I knew she meant this much to you, I coulda rearranged somethin'."

"Yeah, she should have," I said, pounding the beer and leaving Knox to go grab another one.

I noticed Kylee on the dance floor with the girls. She was dancing with her hips moving back and forth, and my dick started to get hard. The damn thing never cooperated with my heart, which was back home in San Diego. I hated loving Kylee. She was fucking beautiful, no denying it; but Harper drove me mad, like a damn cowboy not able to ride his horse, mad. I loved Kylee, but not in the way I desired Harper.

I looked around the club and realized this wasn't home anymore for me. I missed Harper's sexy little ass in those yoga shorts she always wore, and her perky tits, which spilled over her V-neck shirts. I shot her a quick text, reminding her how much I needed her here.

At club. Miss you. Come here.
Need you. Now.
Xoxo
Ry

Kylee got my attention and waved me over to the group of our friends. Fuck it! I'd at least try to enjoy myself. Maybe Kylee and I could get along...as friends.

We danced together, and every time she tried something I pushed her away; but for the most part, it was chill. Knox and I competed with each other to see who could out drink the other, and I won. I still had it in me, but the rest of the night started to blur around midnight, when my head was spinning, and Knox and I cheersed to our third shot of Jim Beam.

At 2am, the club closed, and we headed back to Knox's place. I was shitfaced and needed to crash. I told 'em goodnight, but everyone else was too hammered to even notice, so I just walked to my room. It was hot, too fucking hot in Texas.

When I got to the room, I stripped off my clothes and passed out in bed. I didn't hear anything else from that point. The house could be burning down for all I knew, I was too drunk.

***

My brain was pounding against my skull. Fuck this. I was hammered last night. I needed a Motrin and Gatorade…yesterday. I got up and grabbed the glass sitting next to me. Suddenly, I felt someone's body rustling next to mine, and could hear someone moan.

Who?

What?

The fuck is going on?

I messed up so badly if it's who I thought it was. I needed to get the hell outta here. I turned around and saw Kylee's naked ass tangled in the sheets. I couldn't remember sleeping with her. I looked around for the used condom, but thankfully didn't find any, unless my dumbass didn't use one. Goddamn it. Fuck!

I pounded my fists into the nightstand, which immediately jerked Kylee out of her sleep.

"What the fuck are you doin' in here, Kylee? Put your clothes on, now."

This was a complete betrayal to Harper. I don't know what I would do or how I would begin to tell her. *Goddamn it, Ryder, you fucked up,* I groaned to myself in frustration.

"Chill out, Ryder. I know you're beating yourself up, but I had to sleep in here. Mom kicked me out of my room because I was too loud and drunk with Evelyn in there. I have a shirt on." She motioned to her shirt, which she pulled down past her ass.

"In fact, I even placed this pillow barrier between us. Don't worry. Please."

I noticed the pillows that were placed in a line down the bed. Maybe this wasn't that bad. God, I needed to tell Harper anyways. I didn't want to hurt her, and this would. I needed to call her…now.

"Leave, Kylee. I will meet you downstairs in 10."

"Ry, its okay. I promise. She'll understand," she said apologetically.

"There was almost 30 other rooms you could have passed out in. It will never happen again." I gestured to the door and she walked out.

I grabbed my phone, and my insides were about to explode, but I needed to call Harper now.

It rang...once…twice…

"Good morning, baby." I was such an ass. I was going to ruin her day. Why does it always happen that I can fuck up so royally?

"I need to talk to you." I was direct.

"Shit, what did you do? Ryder, I swear to God…"

"Listen to me before you go freakin' out on me. I was drunk last night with Knox. I came home and I went to sleep. Kylee couldn't go back to her room because she was drunk, so she crashed here."

"WHAT. THE. FUCK?!" Harper screamed into the phone.

"No, I swear to you. She had clothes on and put pillows in the middle of the bed. She didn't do anything. I didn't do anything. I could never. Please, Harper, believe me." At this point, I didn't care that I was begging for her forgiveness. I never wanted to bring Kylee here. The urge to reach through the phone and wrap my arms around her was so strong; I had to hold myself down just to get composed.

"There wasn't a couch or another bed she could've slept on?"

"I don't know! I swear to you right now, I was so drunk I didn't even hear her come in. I was passed out, dead to the world."

"That doesn't make anything right, Ryder. Why do you do this to me?" She sounded hurt. I made her feel pain.

The world was coming down around me. I was a disappointment to her. I couldn't live with myself knowing her heart was breaking and there was next to nothing I could do about it.

"I didn't mean to. I promise, Harper. Come out here. Come today. I need you, please."

"I'll think about it, Ryder," she said, and clicked the phone off. I guess it was better than a no.

I stripped down and got in the adjoining shower. I was becoming my father. A miserable prick who messed up in every way possible. A man who hated anyone but himself. I needed to stop. I needed Harper more than she could even imagine. I needed to taste her, to make love to her, to feel her right next to me. I loved her, so why was I always messing up around Kylee?

When I got dressed, I headed downstairs; Knox laughed and poured me a cup of black coffee.

"Big day tomorrow, bro," I said, looking over at Kylee and Savannah, who were playing with Evelyn.

"Yeah. I can't wait." He stared at Savannah. He loved her, needed her, and did everything for her; so why couldn't that be me?

"You nervous? Ever think you'll fuck this all up?"

I was hoping he could indirectly give me something to go off of.

"Never. When you love someone, you don't fuck up, you just know."

Shit. He was right. I needed to get out of here, clear my head. Get away from Kylee and all this shit. I knew exactly where I needed to go. I went to Evelyn, kissed her on her head, and asked Knox if I could borrow his Lambo. He threw me the keys and I headed out the door.

I couldn't deal with knowing how badly I'd fucked up with Harper. This wasn't the first time, but I'd make damn sure it would be the last. I was pissing the second best thing—behind Evelyn—to happen to me away.

I revved the engine, holding the stick shift in my hand as I pressed the gas. Damn, I needed a car like this. I sped down his driveway and onto the street, driving out of Sugar Land and back towards Houston. The top was down and I could feel the wind around me, but I didn't give a crap. I was on a mission. I knew where I needed to go.

I drove to Reliant Stadium and sped past the employee entrance, flashing my old badge. It wasn't a game day, so it was quiet. I pulled up to my old spot, and threw the car into park. I missed the feeling of exhilaration, knowing you're approaching the field. Ironically, it was eerily quiet, but I could imagine the pass coming down the middle as I dove to catch the ball and running it to a touchdown.

I walked onto the field, explaining to the security guard who I was and how I was here for old time's sake. The green Astroturf under my feet crunched, and the white lines chalked on the field had me aching to play. I loved the game. It was my life here. The guys were my family; the field was my home.

I looked up into the now-empty stands and could feel the crowd roar around me, chanting the team's mantra, and screaming my name. One game. One game was all it took to lose everything. I never blamed Kylee for losing in that game, but it was the day I found out Evelyn was mine. I was distracted, didn't know where the rush was coming from, and ended up on the bottom of the pile.

I could almost hear the roar of the crowd as I walked to the sidelines where the team would sit. I glanced up, knowing Pat, my agent, would always be to the top right, usually glaring at me…that asshole.

I remembered spring training, and going out and getting shitfaced after we completed sets of sprints. It was a dream, but that's all it would ever be: a dream.

I walked around for a while, and sat down in one of the bleachers in the first row. I really needed Harper here with me. It wasn't the same without her, and I was sick of messing up.

"Set up, man," I said out loud. I was being an ass and imitating the same thing my ole' man did. He had a one-track mind, nothing but his goals, his dreams, and his life he imagined for me mattered. It wasn't the same without her, and I was sick of fucking up.

I pulled out my phone and sent a text to Harper.

I'm sorry I always fuck up.
I need you here. Ticket is waiting for you.
Please come.
Ry

I needed to touch her skin, and let her small, warm hands wrap around my back to comfort me. I wanted her to run her fingers through my hair, reminding me everything would be fine. I realized in that moment that didn't love Kylee; sometimes my dick was confused, but I found her attractive, and that was it. She was the mother of my Evie. She gave me Evelyn, and the emotion I was feeling towards her was appreciation, not love.

When my phone didn't respond, I shoved it back into my jeans and got up to leave. I needed to confront good ole' Pops to move on from all of this. I couldn't deal with the fact that I was slowly becoming him by mowing out everyone in my life. I needed to tell him I wasn't going to be with Kylee, or with his fucking law firm. He had to move on from this gross idea he had of his loser son.

I needed to talk to Kylee and figure out where she was going. I couldn't have her here and me be stuck in San Diego. I needed to figure something out. As I got to the car, I dialed her number.

"Hey," she said coldly.

"Meet me at my parents," I directed.

"Your who?" she asked, as if she wasn't sure she heard me correctly.

"I need you to meet me at my parents. Now," I ordered.

"Okay, okay. Be there in an hour."

I couldn't believe I was going there. I was facing the man who hated his own son for years. The family who emancipated their own child for his entire adult life. I was doing it for Harper, because I knew if she was here she would push me to face them. I was doing it because I needed to get it off my chest. I was doing it for my daughter, my love, and myself.

I drove to their house, knowing the route from memory.

Chapter 6

Harper

My hands were shaking violently, and I blinked through clouds of tears. The darkness seeped deep into my pores, and I felt engulfed by a blanket of fatigue. My eyelids were heavy and I needed to blink, but my eyes wouldn't open. It's as if they were completely glued together. I was stuck and scared. Fever broke throughout my body, and my fingers kept flicking at my skin.

My mind was hovering over a huge white bed, and in the middle of it were two entangled bodies, molded together, going at it. She had flowing blonde hair and he had deep black hair that was pulled back as she grabbed it, then shoved her hips down over his dick. He grunted out in pleasure, and all I could do was stand there and watch the whole thing happen.

Nothing came out of my mouth, not even a small shrill. She was bouncing up and down on him while she moaned again. He was chanting her name.

"Kylee. Kylee. Kylee." He kept repeating over and over again. I felt my worst fear come to life as she began to cum continuously. They both cried out together in a mutual orgasm as I sunk to the floor, hugging my knees tight against my chest.

I was watching the love of my life fuck his ex-wife on the bed we could have just made love in. Why hadn't I gone with him? In my imagination, he didn't see me sitting there, listening to him rip one into her again. I kept sitting on the end of the bed, crouched and hugging my knees tightly against my chest. The tears started to drain from my eyes as waterfalls exploded from my face.

When he was done, I heard him kiss her and get up from the bed. He walked right past me where he simply looked down and laughed.

"You sorry little girl. You should have never trusted me." He just laughed and walked on. When he came back, I could hear him rustling in the sheets with her. They were sitting together talking.

"I can't believe you ever thought you loved that girl."

"I know; she was just a notch on my bedpost." He growled in the sexy Texan accent that usually had me moistening my panties in pleasure, but now I was crying in pain. The pain he was causing me felt too familiar. I needed to run, far away from here. I needed to go. I tried to reach for the door and jiggle the handle, but nothing worked. I was stuck.

Help. Someone, please help me. My guilt was manifesting itself. I had tried to hook up with someone at the bar, and now I had to bear witness as the love of my life, the center of my soul, fuck his ex-wife in that bed. The bed we would've shared together as I watched this manifestation of my worst fear come to life. I needed to stop. I needed to run, but I couldn't pick myself up to even think about doing it.

"What a fucking slut," the blonde-haired witch cackled.

"She was just a pathetic little girl who followed me around like a high-maintenance slut."

The air was sucked out of my lungs and I couldn't breathe in or out. Everything was airtight, and my body started convulsing as I moved like I was having a seizure on the floor. I curled up, my back pressed as tight as it would go under the bed and hugged my knees to my chest.

Why was he saying this? Where was the Ryder I knew, and who was this guy here in his place? Gah. I had all these questions that were sitting there unanswered, but all I could zone in on was the giggling happening between the two entwined bodies on the bed above me.

Something told me to run and I ran to the door, looking back at the two figures laughing hysterically at me. They were pointing like a pair of catty teenagers and kept giggling.

"You're never going to get him, honey," she repeated continuously at me between laughs.

"We are done. Finished," he responded in the same dominant voice that once used to turn me on.

I grabbed the handle to the door once again and pushed harder, twisting it over to the left side, then moving it to the right. I grabbed my wrist and pushed harder to force the handle to budge. I pounded on the door, desperately hoping someone would answer and I would be free from this hellish nightmare. I slammed my wrists into the wood door with such force, suddenly I heard a small crack in my wrists as if I had broken something.

When I looked down, I saw my hand turning purple and swelling. Crap, I think I broke my hand, and I was still stuck in this room, which felt as if the walls were closing in on me quickly.

I fell to the floor, and my swollen hand started throbbing. I could feel the pain move from my wrist as it migrated upwards towards the middle of my arm; but the only real pain I felt was the one coming from the betrayal of the man I loved.

I closed my eyes, hoping to blink this all away, and I could feel the darkness seep back into me. I could feel the escalating force of bleakness enter my disembodied soul. If I wasn't sure of myself, how could I have been so sure about our relationship? I was stupid enough to rush into something without thinking. The question is now whether or not I should rush out of it as quickly, or should I try to give it a chance.

Ryder needed me. He was alone in Texas, dealing with the demons he helped me get past, and here I was, selfishly waiting on him while he got lost in his past. He was confused, broken, and frustrated, and I was just sitting here like a piece of shit.

My eyelashes fluttered open, and I saw the scratches that reappeared on my wrists. I immediately got up and saw small trickles of blood that had seeped into the threads of the sheets.

It was all a dream, Harper. It was all a dream.

I needed to go save my relationship before it was too lost to find.

Chapter 7

Ryder

I revved the car and moved down the street, but something was stopping me. I needed to face Pops to show him I am a man, a father, and something he will never be to me. I needed to do this to become a better man for Harper. Be the love of her life that protected her. Kylee had to leave, and I had to tell 'em all. That was it.

If Kylee needed to take Evelyn away from me and stay in Houston, so be it. If she thought that would make everything better, I would make it work. I would show my father he wasn't in control of his twenty-eight year old son's life. Done.

I pulled into the circle driveway and parked next to Mom's Mercedes. I loved her, but I didn't know her. I was raised by Rosetta, the housekeeper. I remember calling Rosetta 'Mom' for years until I realized, the stranger I shared a house with was actually my mom. How many fuckin' parent/teacher conferences did they attend?

I saw Kylee pull in beside me.

"Evelyn here?" I asked, prayin' she wasn't so she wouldn't have to witness this shit.

"No, I left her back with Mom and Savannah," she said.

"Thank you," I responded.

"This is a big thing you're doing, Ry. I am proud of you, you know?"

I stopped her and grabbed her shoulders.

"Kylee. You and I will never happen ever again. I love Harper. I know that hurts you, because I was an ass to you when we were together, but I don't want to fuck this up with her. I need to do this, because I don't know where else I would be without her and Evelyn. Please, just accept that."

Her eyes pierced mine as I finally lifted my hands from her shoulders.

"I know, Ry. Trust me; I know. I don't think that means we can't be friends. As much as you want to cut me out, and you hate me for what I did by getting her pregnant on purpose, that will never happen. You're too much of an amazing father for it to happen."

"Don't stay here then, Kylee," I pleaded with her, begging her to not uproot everyone.

"Let's just go inside. You ready?" she asked, knowing this moment was hard for me. I needed Harper here with me, but she wasn't picking up my calls.

I need you. Going to see my parents today.
Texas. Now.
Ry

The message was short, but I needed her to understand the urgency in the matter. She had no other option. She had to be here. I grabbed whatever balls I had left and walked into the house, knowing I was doing this all for her. This was to make myself a better man for her, and for my daughter. I needed to face this asshole and try to understand why he did what he did.

"Let's just go," I said, pushing her away from me and walked towards the door.

The door was a foot taller than me, and I was 6'4". It was fuckin' obnoxious at how ornate it was. When Rosetta answered the door, I swooped her up off her feet as she shrilled.

"Oh, Ryder," she cried between spins. Rosetta was still the same, sweet, small lovely lady I remembered, but with a few more years on her.

"You came back!" she exclaimed when I finally put her down.

"Just for a wedding, Rose. I need to speak to Mom and Pops; they 'round?" I asked, inhaling the scent of rice and beans coming from the kitchen.

The house was fuckin' huge. In no way did three people ever need this much space. There were more people who worked on the house on a daily basis than who actually lived in it. Pops liked showin' off his wealth to his friends, so he drove fast cars and bought big houses; that was his way of life.

Rosetta quickly nodded her head and ushered us into the sitting room. Yes, a fuckin' sitting room.

"Thank you, dear," Kylee smiled at Rosetta, who quickly left to get us somethin' to drink.

"I love your house, Ry."

"You gotta stop calling me that." I sat on the uncomfortable couch, not the kind of couch you would watch a Sunday night football game on, but something your Nana would cover in plastic. I tried shifting around, but the thing wouldn't get any better, so I just gave up.

"I'm sorry. I don't get why we can't just…" Kylee started, but was interrupted by a small cough that could only announce my mother's presence in the room.

"Ryder, darling. You have finally decided to grace us with your presence after all these years."

I got up, in proper southern respect, but didn't approach her. She looked like Cruella Deville from those kids movies.

"I need to talk to you and Pops. Where is he?" I didn't care to make small talk with these people. These were the people who birthed me, not the ones who took care of me.

Rosetta quickly came back with some iced waters and lemonades, and sat them on the middle table.

"Thanks, Rose." I smiled and then flashed straight back to the woman who I was suppose to call Mom.

"He's on his way down, son. He is just finishing up a conference call. You know he is just so busy because you won't help him out."

"Don't start," I bellowed, forcing the silence back into the room.

Mom sat there, twiddling her thumbs around, waiting for Pops to come down from his conference call. I could hear the incessant tick of the clock on the wall that continued, driving my nerves crazy.

I was getting pissed off more and more by the minute. I glanced over at Kylee, who was shifting nervously in her seat. She knew how I felt about this, and how I was going to explode when Pops came down.

"Hello, Mrs. Kent," she said, trying to deter the conversation.

"Kylee, dear, how are you?" my mother asked her as if nothing happened.

This is what she was good at, making conversation about things that really don't matter in life.

"I'm fine."

"How is that little girl of yours?" she asked, which frankly, pissed me off. She knows Evelyn's name, and knows very well that she is also mine.

"Say her name and recognize she is my daughter." I wiped my palms on the couch and kept 'em tucked under me, otherwise I wouldn't be able to keep myself from wailing on her.

"You were the one who planned her, remember?" I screamed this time.

"I did not tell Kylee to go off her…protection." She wasn't able to say birth control. God forbid she say something so classless.

"Well, to be fair, Mrs. Kent, both you and my mother pressured me to settle down and get off of it. While you didn't directly say it, I felt forced to, because y'all made me feel I was going to amount to some useless human being if I didn't end up with Ryder. Not that I'd ever regret Evie, I just…" Kylee spoke up for the first time. I turned to look at her, shocked she even said somethin'.

I spoke up, defendin' her, "She's right, *Mom*. Neither of us regret Evelyn, but damn, y'all were conniving."

Something about her was changing, hopefully. Maybe she was trying to work things out anyways. Who knew, but hopefully we could get things hashed out for Evelyn.

"What's the commotion in here?"

Pops.

His always knew how to make an entrance just at the right moment. He was in his typical Armani suit. I can't remember a day he changed from the damn thing. When I stood up, it was like looking in a mirror that aged you a couple years. I hated that we looked so much alike. Damn.

"Father." I shook his hand and he sat down next to Mom.

"What brings you back here? This is quite a surprise," he said in his business-like manner. It was always about business with him.

"I need to talk to y'all. Get this off my chest before I go back to San Diego. I am here for Kayden Knox's wedding."

"Ah, yes. He is marrying that Livingston girl, isn't he?" Pops asked.

"Yup."

"Good for him, finally settling down. It's about time one of you settled down," he griped. "What are you here to talk about then, son?"

"I need your blessing to move on. I am sick of feeling like a damn disappointment in your eyes. I want everyone in this room to leave me alone about the damn law school thing. It ain't ever going to happen," I drawled.

"Son, you know you need to provide for your family; and here you are, gallivanting around town while leaving your wife and daughter at home," he started ranting before Kylee and I quickly interrupted at the same time.

"Ex-wife," we said in unison.

"Either way. Y'all are family, and you don't leave family for dust."

"How can you even begin to say that? You left me behind!" I screamed, my fists pounding against the side of the couch, making Kylee jump.

"You left on your own accord, son. I told you what was important in life, and it wasn't football. Look at how that dream turned out."

"Fuck you, Pop. Fuck. You."

"I will not have that language in this house, you hear me, Ryder Andrew?" my mother interrupted.

"Seriously, though," I began, "how can you guys sit here and act like everything is perfectly okay? It's not. You forced Kylee to have a fuckin' baby with me when I wasn't ready to have a kid. You disowned your own fuckin' kid because he was a goddamn pro footballer."

"Son, no one forced you guys to engage in intimate behaviors, and no one left you behind." My dad laughed with a devilish look on his face, as if something in this conversation was funny.

Mom chimed in, "You were just acting a little silly, Ryder. Who plays football as a profession? Seems all a little bit ridiculous, if you ask me."

"I DID! I played football for a profession, and you guys *knew* I was fuckin' Kylee." I emphasized 'fuck' just to see the look on Mom's face twist with disgust.

"In all fairness," Kylee piped in, "you guys did tell me it was something I should consider doing with the baby and all. I may not agree with the whole football thing, sorry, Ry, but with Evelyn, it was kind of a sucky situation."

"We are sorry, son, if you feel like we forced this on you, but we really wanted the best for you," Mom spoke up.

"It was for the best. It was because you wanted to do the football thing, which we knew was never going to work out. I needed someone to take over the firm for me, and wanted to keep it in the family. It was what you were suppose to do." At least he was telling the truth now.

"Yeah, but that's not what I wanted. You both have royally screwed me up in more ways than you even realize. I have to deal with all this crap about feeling like a shitty father..."

"You are not," Kylee interjected, "don't you ever feel like that."

"But I do. It's how I feel, like I have to be better than Pops. You never see your own granddaughter because y'all don't even care. I don't get how you don't maintain some sort of relationship with her, or your own son for that matter."

"Well, darling, you are all the way in San Diego." Mom shriveled her nose and swiped the wrinkles off her dress. She didn't care; she was simply making up excuses to pretend like she wanted to.

"Then why the fuck would you think having a baby would be a good thing?" My face were red with fury. I wanted to slam something, or someone, against the wall hard enough I could hear the bones in their face crack. I was violently angry with them. Angry they would throw their son to the wolves because he wasn't good enough for them, and then not be there to support him as he raised his daughter like a good man. Moreover, I was pissed they weren't there for me to give me support as their child, a shoulder to cry on when I was young. I don't remember cryin', because if I did, Pops would hand me over to Rosetta. He didn't handle it well, and frankly, I didn't understand why he didn't. When Evie cried, I got an overwhelmin' sense of being needed; it was my duty to be her knight in shinin' armor and make everything better.

"I was so good at football, though. Most families would be proud if their son was an NFL player. I was good at it, and makin' money while doing somethin' I loved."

"But we knew your career would end quickly, Ryder. Football isn't something you play forever, and then what would you do? You had no solid backup plan, and I was ready to retire and hand you a ten-million dollar law firm."

"Did you ever think I wasn't ready to run a ten- million dollar law firm? Y'all ever think I just wanted to do what I was doin'."

"Son, we wanted the best for you; it's what every parent wants."

My fists were balled up tight, and I swear I was going to go fuckin' crazy, sittin' on this couch a minute longer; so I got up, and went to leave.

I had to get outta here. I wanted to kill this son of a bitch who had the balls to call himself my father. He was nothing but a sperm donor for me. And that pathetic excuse for a mother was just someone who formulated a plan to get a vulnerable girl pregnant, just so that I could possibly give them a future, and have a loveless marriage like they had. I swear to God, they were out of their minds.

All the while, I couldn't stop thinking about Harper, who was sitting back in San Diego having to deal with her nightmares and terrors by herself if she was having them. Here I was, thinking this was the worst of my issues, but I was never physically hurt by these people, so it should hurt less.

The neglect I got from my parents, the constant ignorance they had for me when I was growing up, hurt me. I would never actually admit it to a crowd of people, but why couldn't I have real parents who cared about their own son's life. No, Harper and I were so much more alike than I cared to acknowledge. We were two broken people walking on this earth, who just so happened to find each other. I needed her here with me now. At this point, I could care less about the wedding. I needed Harper. I needed to show here I could be the man my Pops wasn't to my Mom. I wanted to be the man and father I never had.

Just being the way she is changed my life. She could walk in with her tiny ass shorts on, and a plain t-shirt, and I could be instantly turned on. She could simply speak, and I was mesmerized. I needed her in my life. She was the crutch I used to survive. The only piece of happiness in this whole fucked up world we lived in.

'Til this day, I could not imagine what she had to go through with…him. I refused to utter his name without spitting it out in disgust, a useless waste of space. Who would ever lay their hands on a woman, especially Harper? I couldn't fathom that the piece of shit still breathes.

I would never understand the abuse she had to go through on a daily basis when she was with him, but the neglect I felt from my parents was despicable. I held them on the same level I held Tye, and the things he did to Harper. My parents outright ignored me for my entire life growing up, and even since I've been grown.

Still, as I was heading out, I heard Kylee shout my name, and I turned around to her standing over my parents. She was big into southern tradition, so I hadn't actually ever seen her stand up to my parents. I was surprised she said anything in the conversation at all. She was normally the one who sat behind and just took it. I'm being an ass, but it's true. She did what she was told, and had a kid when she knew neither one of us was ready. She did it and moved to San Diego when I told her that's where I was headin'. She married me just 'cause that's what sshe was 'supposed to do', so I was taken aback when she even remotely spoke up.

"Stay, Ryder. I have something to say." She looked over at my parents as I stood by the doorframe, afraid to move any closer than I was.

"Listen, Mr. and Mrs. Kent; I really do respect y'all, as you have known my family for years; but what both of you did was messed up. You took two vulnerable kids looking to find themselves in this world and shoved them together. Mrs. Kent, you and my mom told me it was safer if I wasn't on birth control, and that it was a good idea to try to conceive with Ryder because he would be able to support me. That ultimately only caused both of us deeper amounts of pain, and we were too young to deal with it all. I love Evelyn, and wouldn't trade her for anything; but we weren't meant to be together, and we definitely weren't meant to have a child together."

She was now looking at me with something in her eyes I haven't seen in years: remorse. I heard my dad cough, and she quickly turned back to them and continued, before he could get a word in edgewise.

"You never treated your son like he was worth anything, and neither did I. We all thought football was going to be just this big hobby of his, but he wanted to make a career out of it; now he loves surfing, from what Evie tells me. You both either need to support him, or just leave him alone and let him live his life."

"He is with this woman who loves him for who he is. No offense, Mrs. Kent, but she loves him more than you have ever even liked him. She is better for him than any of us in this room, and we have to all let him go to just move on. I don't propose some sort of magical resolve of this issue, but I think we all should give him the permission to move on with his life."

I looked at her and almost felt like breaking down. As a man, I would never admit to crying, but what Kylee said was true. I didn't need their permission to fix the problems, because I tried for twenty-eight years to fix 'em with nothin' from them. I needed to move on from 'em and the pain they cause me every fuckin' day. I needed to get on so I could show Harper what healing looked like, what being a man and a boyfriend looked like, because that's all I have ever wanted: to be in love with someone who loved me back.

I fucked all those women in college, and even Kylee, just to know what was like to feel love, even if it was just the physical kind. It's why Harper did what she did, sleepin' around and shit. I understood her more by trying to get through to my parents. I understood how she struggled everyday trying to fix a problem that wasn't fixable. I was sitting here trying to mend a fence that wasn't broken. It just wouldn't work…period.

"Kylee is right. There is nothing to fix here." I started to walk towards the front door and heard my father come behind me.

"Ryder Andrew, listen to me. I just want what is best for you."

"I hear you keep saying that, but I don't see your actions proving it. In fact, all you're doing is sittin' here lecturin' me, but I don't see anything comin' out of this."

"We aren't bad parents, Ryder; it hurts your mother when you say we were terrible to you. We never laid a hand on you, gave you everything you needed and could possibly think of. All we asked for in return was for you to better yourself by working with my company."

"Why are you so hell-bent on me workin' as a lawyer, Dad? I don't want to! Get that through your thick skull. That is not somethin' I will ever do," I bellowed at him.

"And to top it all off, while you might not have physically slapped me across the face, your absolute ignorance to what I want to do with my life, or the fact you give zero shits about your granddaughter, is enough for me not to care."

"Of course we care about Evelyn, Ryder. Why aren't you listening to me? You never listen; you always think you are right son. I don't know where you got that trait from, but certainly not from either your mother or myself."

"Because I didn't have a fucking dad growing up, Pops! I didn't get the chance to throw the baseball in the yard after school because no one was here to help me catch it. I had a machine that would, sure, but I wanted that good ole' encouragement from you, my father. You were the man I was supposed to model, but I wanted to do everything opposite from you. I want to do everything you didn't do."

"I am in love, Pops, and I want to move on from all of this so I can show her that I am capable of being the man you aren't."

"Ryder, you will never be a man. You are wasting your life away doing nothing but working at a stupid…coffee place. It's pathetic how you have succumbed to working for people who are much lower than your class. You are useless to us."

"Go to fuckin' hell," I breathed, staring him straight in the eyes. I hated lookin' like this man. I was a carbon copy of him in terms of looks, but he was not even half the man I was.

"We thought you would finally get your act together when Kylee got pregnant. We knew that you two couldn't avoid each other, and it was easy to get Kylee off her birth control, so we figured we'd push her to do it. It would give Kylee a direction in life, and some stability, and you would have a purpose and work for the firm."

"Do you know how disgusting that sounds?" I wanted desperately to walk out the door and never look back, but I wanted to hear what he had to say. I needed to hear it.

"No, it's because I was looking out for you, Ryder. I do not feel that was disgusting at all. I was there for you with what you needed in life, and was trying to look out for you. You had other plans."

"You pushed a vulnerable girl into having sex with me unprotected, knowing very well y'all wanted her to get pregnant. Then you left me high-and-dry with no emotional support when I had the child, simply because I wasn't good enough for you. That, Father, is fucked…up."

"Please do not use that vile language around me or your mother. It will not be tolerated in this house," he screamed, looking at me with no emotional response in him.

"Listen, Pops; I have nothing more to say to you. I was hoping we could come to some resolution from all of this, but it looks like nothing will occur. We are two stubborn people, but I needed to tell you and Mom that you both messed up, and how that affected me. I can't do this anymore with y'all, so I have to let go, move on, and live my life."

"So, why are you here, son? Why come back if we were such terrible people?" I could feel my mother and Kylee walking in from behind us, but I had to get out what I wanted to say before leaving.

"Because I needed to tell you, all of you," I said, pointing at Kylee and Mom behind me, "that I am done with this family. I am over it and movin' on. I will forgive, but never forget the neglect I went through as a kid. I am sorry I was born into this life, but I can't deal with it anymore. I am done. Done, with all of you. I will never set foot in this house again, and I hope y'all are happy with your decisions to leave your son with no emotional support whatsoever."

I continued, "I will never bring Evelyn by and you will never see her again with me; but if you so choose to see her, and Kylee allows it, then fine. I want to move on so I can give the life I never had to a woman who loves me, so that I can be the man you never will be. Goodbye, Mom and Pop. Hope you someday realize the mistakes of your past, but I sure as hell won't be around to remind ya'."

I pushed the door of the house open and saw Rosetta standing on the porch with tears in her eyes. She must've heard what I said, so I walked over to her, and wrapped her in a hug before leaving. Without a wave or a second to let them respond, I left my incubators behind. They were never supportive of me, nor would they even be considered parents. They gave me financial support, but neglected to love or care for me unconditionally, which is what parents are put here to do.

You can't fix what's not meant to work, and it's not worth my time or patience to care about somethin' they see as fine. I had the closure I needed, so it's time to hightail outta here, and get back to Harper and little Evelyn.

Alright. I'll be the bigger man and admit it. I was pissed as hell they weren't going to be parents and we couldn't end things with lollipops and roses, but I got what I had to say out, and that's all I could do; nothing more could be done.

Although, when I left the house as pissed off as I was that I couldn't change their hardened ways, I felt relieved I didn't have to be the one to deal with them again. I was glad I got what I had to say out, and hear what I heard. I knew from Kylee what my parents had done, but I'd needed to hear *from them* that they orchestrated the whole pregnancy thing, pressuring Kylee to have sex with me without protection. I needed to hear it from them that they essentially ruined what I had and in turn, my football career, because they wanted me to become "grounded" or some bullshit like that. It sucked, but it just is what it is. I couldn't change what happened.

Whatever. I was just pissed off more than I would have wanted to be. I heard the crunch of the gravel from behind me and heard someone bellow my name.

"Ryder! Wait up, please," Kylee shouted.

"What do you want?" I asked her. While I was glad she finally spoke her mind, we still hadn't talked about her movin' out here, or anything of that sort.

"Would you want to meet me at Sue's Diner? I wanna grab some brisket and talk about things. Please?" She begged.

"I ain't tryin' to get back with you, Kylee, but we do need to talk about you fixin' to move out here, so I'll meet you there. You understand, though, very clearly, I will walk out if you start discussin' getting back together."

"I know, I know. I swear to you, I just wanna talk about Harper, and moving and stuff too." She looked at me with truth in her eyes, so I got in the car, and headed down the driveway. I sped off to meet her at Sue's.

***

We sat in one of those old-timey leather booths and a small elderly lady took our orders. Kylee ordered the brisket sandwich and I got a steak. I needed to be direct after the conversation I had with my parents that drove me crazy.

"What's up? You wanna move here and take Evelyn with ya? You better have a fuckin' plan because I am not playing games with you. I don't have time for any of your childish ways."

"I just stuck up for you, Ry; the least u can do is cut me some slack…damn."

"I just need to know what the fuck I'm suppose to do with my life, and you won't tell me. If I gotta move out here and leave Harper, I have to figure out what I am going to do. Hell, if I have to rent a damn jet to get to her, I will; but I need to figure that out."

"You love her a lot, don't you?" Kylee asked, while playing with her straw with her mouth.

"Yes, Kylee, I really do love her. I don't mean to say I didn't love you, because I did at one point, and always will; but the love I feel for you is different. When I'm with Harper, I feel like I could move mountains to make her happy. She tames me, makes me feel okay about my past, and we help each other. We are just two broken souls that found each other. You aren't broken, Kylee."

"What do you mean?" she asked.

"I mean, you have everything going for you. You aren't broken or damaged in ways that me and Harper are."

"You don't know that! I had a baby when I wasn't ready, and had to deal with you cheating on me and leaving me constantly. I have trust issues with men because of you, Ry."

"But, you come from a good home, a good past, and a decent life. Harper has her demons, and I have mine, and together we work through them."

"She changed you. I can see it. It scared me at first, which is why I think I tried to get back together with you; but seeing you stand up to your parents, I can now see the change she has created in you. You actually spoke up to them. I have known you my whole life, and you were that quiet boy in the corner who just did what he was told, or ran away. Instead, I saw you looking your dad in the eye and telling him off. I was completely impressed, actually, because that was a long time coming. Can I be honest with you?"

I grabbed the mug full of hot coffee and nodded my head so she'd continue.

"I hated my parents for telling me that I *needed* to be with you. I didn't need to be with anyone, but I was scared I was going to amount to some *loser;* so I wanted to make them happy, sort of like you. I didn't mean to get off the pill and get pregnant right away; it just happened. You happened to not be able to pick up any girls that night and came to me. I shouldn't have done it, or I should have told you, and I did fuck up…"

"Don't blame yourself. It took two people to make the baby. It's my fault, too. I shoulda wrapped it up."

"No, you're not listening. It is my fault for lying and thinking everything our parents were saying was fine. It was my fault for seducing you earlier. It's wrong and inappropriate, and I apologize profusely. To be honest, I was completely miserable in San Diego, but I think I might have met somebody who has shown me what I think Harper has shown you."

"Who?"

"I don't want to jinx it right now, because it really is in the early stages of our relationship. It's just new and being developed, but I think he has shown me that you and I aren't meant to be; and just because we have a child together, doesn't necessarily mean we have to be together."

"That's what I have been trying to tell you for a while, Kylee."

"I know, but I am just now realizing it, okay? Sorry, I am a little slow."

"So, you're going to stay in San Diego?" I asked.

"Yeah, I am going to stay with Evelyn. You are an amazing father. I have heard horror stories about women who have children with men and they run away and are never in that child's life. I don't want that, and you aren't like that, so you deserve this shot."

"So do you, Kylee. I want you to be happy as well; but you can't continue meddling in my relationship and tryin' to ruin it."

"I know that now." She started runnin' her fingers through her hair nervously.

"I just need Harper to be okay with you, Kylee. I need you to understand that she will be around Evelyn, and both of you need to sit down and deal with whatever you got goin' on."

"I think that's a good idea. Really, I do. I want to feel comfortable with the woman that's spending so much time around my daughter. I think that's acceptable to ask as well."

"Yes. I have always told you when she is going to be there."

"Well, at least now you can stay with her."

"This isn't just about me, Kylee. It's about you, too. I don't want you stayin' in a place that isn't going to make you happy. Are you happy in San Diego with this new guy around?"

"Yeah, I think I am. He is showing me that sometimes, you can find happiness in the most unexpected place."

"It's the best kind of love, as stupid as I sound," I admitted.

The waitress came over and brought us our food. It was so fuckin' delicious I pounded that thing in seconds. Kylee sat in silence, thinkin' the same thing I was. Everything wasn't exactly fixed like expected, but there was a content feelin' blooming in the air. Everything was okay. Kylee was going to stay in San Diego, which meant I could be around both Harper and Evelyn.

Damn, Harper would love to visit this place. She would get a kick out of the Texas-themed decor, the cowboys, and the waitress with the thick accent. I wished her here…now. Hopefully, she'd reconsidered coming up tomorrow. Otherwise, honest to Pete, I couldn't wait to see her when I got back. Just thinkin' about her made me…fuck.

I couldn't wait to see her perky tits as they bounced up and down. I needed to taste her sweetness in my mouth, licking it up until my mouth felt sore. And damn, I needed her warm, wet mouth around me, moving up and down, driving me even crazier than I already was.

"Ryder?" My daydream was interupted.

"Yeah, what?"

"I just asked if you had spoken to Harper since our meeting with your parents."

I hadn't called her on the drive to the diner because I turned my phone off and shoved it in my pocket. When Kylee reminded me, I pulled it out and started it back up. I noticed a bunch of texts that were coming in.

"Are we clear then, Kylee, that we are nothing more than just two parenting friends? Everything's okay?"

"Yeah. We both have our own relationships we are working on, so I think we are better than just okay, Ryder. I think we've finally figured out what we are good at doing, being parents and not lovers."

I nodded and quickly paid the bill. We both took off heading back to Sugar Land to spend some time with Evelyn before the big wedding tomorrow. I texted Harper again with no response. I prayed to God she wasn't mad at me for what I told her earlier, about sleeping next to Kylee. I don't know what I would do without that woman in my life.

Chapter 8

Harper

I was scared something was going to happen between Ryder and Kylee in Texas. Even more scared because Ryder had texted me about going to visit his parents. I knew he had to have been with Kylee, but I don't understand why he would do something that big unless something between him and Kylee happened. I knew he was with Kylee because she was staying at her parents right by his parent's house. They had talked about going there and talking to his parents for a while now, so I figured this was bound to happen. Kind of put two and two together if that makes any sense. Ryder hated his parents, so why was he going to see them? Something must have happened.

The fact that Ryder felt the need to call me and tell me Kylee slept in his bed freaked me out even more. But beyond all this, I was having my nightmares again with no one here to protect me. I felt completely alone. It was only mid-afternoon, so I knew I had time to call Skye and talk to her before she went into class. I didn't have class on Fridays, but Skye did.

I pulled out my phone and dialed her number.

"Hey, Harp!" she squealed over the phone in her usual perky manner.

"I need your help. Come over after class?" I asked directly, not wanting for her to be late for anything.

"Uh-oh. You 'kay?" she asked me; this time her voice was more laden with concern.

"Yeah, I just don't know what to do."

"Okay. I just got to go to this class, but I promise I will be there in an hour. Love ya." She clicked off the phone, and I got out of bed and went to take a shower.

I felt disoriented from the reality I was living in. I was numb, almost, to the fact my boyfriend was sleeping in the same bed as his ex-wife. It should have hurt me more than it did now; but it didn't, and I wasn't sure why.

A part of me knew I should go to Texas and figure something out with him, but the other part wanted nothing to do with it and live my life pretending like the phone call didn't happen. I wanted to run away from all of this and forget my problems. After I got dressed in a white skater-style sundress, I heard a loud knock on the door.

"Open the door, Harper Mae!" I heard Skye bellow from the other side.

I ran to get the door and opened it to my flustered best friend.

"How can you call me and just tell me you need help right before I was going into class? You know my class schedule; I couldn't even concentrate during the lecture!" She shrilled at me before plopping down on the couch, with her book bag making a loud thump on the ground.

"I need to talk to you about Ryder. I don't know what to do and I'm freaking out." She looked at me in surprise when I told her. Normally, we didn't talk about guys, unless they were her guys we were chatting about. I didn't like talking too much about my personal life, so this was a big step for me.

"Oh. Well, what's going on?" She propped up on her elbows and stared at me straight in the eye.

"It's Kylee—" was all I needed to say before teardrops started to form in my eyes.

I began telling Skye everything, about how Kylee wanted to move to Texas, and how Ryder was acting differently before he left. I told her that I knew he loved me, but I felt like something was off. I thought maybe he was stressed or something, but wasn't exactly sure what was going on. I hadn't spoken to him in a while and knew he was planning on going to his parent's place, and what a big deal that was for him. I told her all about how he called me earlier that day and told me he slept in the same bed as Kylee, but there was no sex.

Skye just simply stared at me the entire time, listening to my entire word-vomit as I spit out how I felt about the whole thing. When I finished, she finally pitched in.

"I know Ryder loves you, but the thing with Kylee is wrong. Regardless if he is stressed or whatever, she could have slept on the couch or done something differently. You need to go there…today. I know we just started school, but you could fly out tomorrow morning and get there just in time for the wedding. I understand where he is coming from with his family, as should you. He had to go over there and deal with all that drama; I am sure he needs you, or someone, and he is searching for the nearest comfort."

"I can't simply go over there, Skye; it's much more complicated than that. I have my last day of work at Rita's tomorrow, anyways. I also have a ton of schoolwork I have to do, even though it's only been the first week of classes."

I was a self-professed bookworm and nerd. The first day of classes stressed me out more than finals week, because I needed to get everything organized and started. I also needed to prove to myself that I wasn't becoming dependent on Ryder. I felt as if I was getting too close to him; because our relationship felt rocky as it was, I didn't want to get too close only to have to run away later.

"Well, then, how about you come out tonight with me and Jayson? He is finally back from his trip, and we both want to celebrate by going to The Grove or something."

The Grove was one of the clubs I first met Ryder at without even knowing. I can remember that moment vividly. His hands sliding down my swaying hips, then cautiously skimming over my throbbing core; his body moving slowly, then gyrating quickly to the beat of the music. Damn, I missed him.

"I guess I can go out, but it's already pretty late; you wanna just get ready here and then head out?" I glanced at the clock and discovered we had been talking for a while now, and the sun had finally set in the sky.

"Anything for you! I just have to text Jayson and let him know the plan." She quickly pulled out her phone while I ordered us some Chinese take-out. I grabbed a couple outfits from my closet and we played dress up as if we were a couple of five-year-olds. I forgot about texting Ryder again, and left my phone at home when we finally left the house.

By 8pm, we were at Skye's penthouse, fully dressed to go out and enjoying some of Jayson's infamous cocktails that he had prepared. We were sitting on her balcony because the night was warmer than usual.

"Hey, Harper. Guess who is coming?" Jayson directed at me.

"Who?" I asked, quite curious, but thinking it was probably some of Skye's sorority sisters.

"Do you remember my buddy Nate? He was here one day when me and Skye first started hanging out a couple months ago, before you met Ryder?"

"Oh sure, I remember him fine." I knew exactly who they were talking about. It was the night I met Ryder on the dance floor. I almost started talking to Nate, but was easily distracted by the dance floor and didn't get a chance to get to know him.

"He's coming, and he hasn't stopped talking about you since he met you."

"Jayson," Skye squealed, "you know she is in a relationship with another man. You can't be setting her up with anyone else. Ryder would just kill you!"

"Baby, I am not setting her up with anyone. I just wanted to let her know he was coming, and that he had the hots for her; that's all." Jayson said.

"Thanks, Jayson, but Skye is right. I am not looking for anything right now. I have everything that I could ever need…or handle."

As if his ears were ringing, Nate stepped into the apartment. As we heard the balcony door slide open, we all turned towards him. He was handsome in a very preppy sort of way. If I wasn't involved with Ryder, I might have even considered giving him a second chance, but it wasn't enough for me. I needed a man who needed me, and that certainly wasn't Nate. Nate was all too consumed with himself, which was obvious when he walked into any room and started smiling a cocky grin.

"What's up guys?" He said as he marched out and grabbed one of the extra drinks. He went around the table, high-fived Jayson, kissed Skye on the cheek, and when he got over to me, he moved slowly and whispered something delicately in my ear.

"Letting you go was my worst mistake."

I just held a fake smile and continued what I was saying to Skye, blatantly ignoring him. After an hour or so, we all got up to go to the club and jumped into Skye's town car.

When we got to The Grove, it was completely packed; luckily Skye had gotten us a table in the VIP section. It was dark inside, and there was a female DJ in the elevated DJ booth in the right hand corner. There were tons of VIP booths on the left-hand side, which were for bottle service only. There was a long, illuminated bar down the center of the club, and a large dance floor in front of it. It was very exclusive, and the line to get in was over two blocks long. I couldn't imagine what Skye spent to get us a VIP table, but it had to have been in the thousands. A server came over with buckets of Grey Goose Vodka, Bacardi, and mixers.

"Cheers to seeing old friends again." Nate raised his glass and we all clinked. As the alcohol burned down my throat, I realized I hadn't thought of Ryder in a while, but the thought of him spending tonight with Kylee made me take another shot…or two…or three.

"Damn girl, you really know how to pound those," Nate said, completely enamored.

"Just trying to ignore some shit that's going on right now," I said truthfully.

"Aren't we all?" He beckoned with his glass, we said cheers, and I threw more booze down my throat.

I wasn't in the mood to dance, but Jayson and Skye had gone off to join the crowded dance floor, while Nate stayed behind and chatted.

I found out that he was part of his dad's consulting business, and we talked about the incessant perfect weather San Diego offers, which club was actually the hottest, and why cranberry-vodka was the perfect female drink.

It was actually quite enjoyable, but for some reason, I felt wrong. I felt as though I was emotionally cheating on Ryder by talking to Nate and laughing with him. Skye and Jayson were nowhere to be found, and my phone was stuck in a drawer in my room…back at home.

"So, you seeing anyone?" I figured this dreaded question was going to come up at some point. Why couldn't men have a light-hearted conversation without thinking about getting in your pants?! This is why I used to use men for what they used women for: sex.

"Yes, I am actually seeing someone pretty great," I responded taking him aback a little bit. I think he had assumed we were flirting. I was simply trying to make light conversation with a male.

"Oh, wow. That's a surprise, but congrats."

"Why is that a surprise?" I asked curiously.

"Because I had just assumed we were flirting together and things were going good. When Jayson invited me here, I figured it was because you wanted to see me or something."

Ohhhh kay, cocky asshole.

"Yeah, no. I am happy."

"Are you really happy if you are sitting here flirting with me?" He inquired, looking at me with a grim expression on his face.

Suddenly, the room around me felt like it was moving a hundred miles a minute. I started to stand up straight, but my legs weren't responding with my brain, and I felt myself collide with the table. The last thing I remembered was hearing was a muffled "boom" as I cracked my head on the table and fell to the floor..

It felt as if I was being transported to a different world—or a new place. But maybe it wasn't very new after all.

***

It was dark inside the room, and felt so familiar. The boy was crying over in the corner as blood poured from his arms. He had the same familiar features I could point out from afar. His body was contorted in the corner so no one could see him. I felt like I needed to rush over there and save him, but nothing around me was quite right. Everything was moving in slow motion and I was trapped, unable to do anything.

"What are you doing?" I tried to scream from where I was, but he couldn't hear me over the sobs that spilled from his mouth.

"I am so sorry, baby; I never meant to hurt you. Please forgive me." He turned over and looked at me while he was crying. I was stuck, as if my feet were locked in quicksand.

"It's okay. You don't have to hurt yourself," I repeated over and over, until finally, he turned and looked at me with a blank stare.

"Yes, I do," he said, as he took the razor and sliced his wrist again and again, making little slices and marks in even rows on his right wrist.

"Please, stop. This isn't right; please, stop," I screamed at him, trying desperately to get over to him, but still locked in place.

"You shouldn't have left me. I never meant to lay a hand on you, you know that, right?" he cried, and I wanted to feel nothing for him, but my heart felt heavy, and the guilt was cripplingly present.

"I'm sorry, baby; I will never leave you again. But will you please stop hurting yourself?" I begged, now in the corner where I finally was able to sink down to his height onto the moldy and crusty carpet.

"I loved you. Why didn't you love me back?" he cried.

I finally realized it was Tye I was talking to, but it wasn't the Tye I remembered. He had aged a few years, and there were heavy wrinkles lining his face. I could never forget the face of the man who abused me for four years; but this guy looked older, as if life took him for a ride.

The stubble on his face was starting to become more of a beard, and the black bags under his eyes were heavy. His hair was longer now, and slicked back, as if he hadn't gotten it cut in years and had forgotten to take a shower in a while. It wasn't a hair product slicking it back, but the grease of an unwashed person. His hands were rugged, and there were pockmarks all over them. You could see the lines of scars marring his wrists where he had previously taken a razor blade to them. We were in the same house we lived in during high school. I remembered the same crying sun mural on the wall, and the mold that covered the carpets and walls. It was pathetic, this man who took everything away from me lived the same life in the same place as he always had. He had never moved away or moved on.

"I had to leave. Otherwise, I was going to be stuck here!" I cried out desperately.

"You didn't have to go anywhere. You didn't have to go, damnit!" he screamed, this time getting up from his corner.

The blood now started pouring out of his hands as he moved closer towards me. I felt so small in the corner as he towered over me, creeping towards me at a turtle's pace.

"You left me for him, Harper. You left me for a guy who doesn't even love you back. A man who would rather be with his past than be with you. You're pathetic. You know that, right?"

Tears welled in my eyes and I finally felt the need to release and cry. The emotions were stirring in my chest and I didn't know how to feel. I was confused, hopeless, and helpless. I couldn't move or open my eyes. I tried to count backwards from ten, but it didn't help, and I was still in the same room. I tried to fight the numb feeling that washed over me, but it was too strong, and I felt disconnected from my body. I was pushed away from where I was disembodied from the physical person crouching in the corner.

"I had to move on. He loves me, Tye; he really loves me." I tried to reason with him, but there was no reasoning with the devil.

"No, he doesn't. He doesn't love you like I loved you. Look where he is now. He is in Texas with his ex-wife and doesn't care about you. He is sleeping in the same bed as his her and went to see his parents without telling you what happened. He is doing all of this so he can move out there and leave you behind. You will always be left behind with him."

No, this couldn't be true. Tye was messing with my head. This couldn't happen. There was no truth to any of this. Ryder needed me. Everything coming from Tye's lips had to have been lies.

"You're lying. He is just busy with the wedding. He loves me."

"He may love you, baby girl, but he will never love you the way I did. I loved you with everything I had. I only hurt you because you hurt me, and I was mad at you. I would never do it again." He kept approaching me, the blood running from his wrists were trickling on the carpet as he left a trail behind him.

"No. You are nothing like him, Tye. You are nothing like Ryder. He would never intentionally hurt me. No, you are wrong."

"You must not love him *enough* if you were sitting at a club trying to hook up with another guy…twice. This is the second time it happened, and you are doing nothing to stop it." He was now towering over me, and he began to crouch down to face me as I huddled in the corner clutching myself as tight as I could.

"You are wrong. You are nothing but a stupid whore."

I cried and felt a warm sensation wash over my face as the familiar stinging of a slap echoed throughout my body. I shut my eyes as tightly and prayed nothing would go further.

I needed Ryder. Where was he, and why wasn't he here right now? I wasn't sure if I was going to be able to get out of this nightmare without him. He was always the one to wake me up and protect me, but here I was, stuck and unable to leave. I needed Ryder with me now. I didn't know what to do or how to leave.

There was no way Ryder could have been with Kylee. He loved me and protected me. He let me stay at his place and told me everyday how much he desired our undeniable attraction. He told me I was the center of his being, so there must be some truth to it all. I needed him.

Get me out of here.

***

"Harper?" Skye cried, while shaking me almost violently.

I took a deep breath in and realized I was outside, where the cool, fresh air was surrounding me. I managed to slow my breathing and cautiously open my eyes to the florescent lighting of the club's parking lot.

"What?" I asked drowsily.

"Are you okay? What happened back there?" I heard a male speak and realized Jayson and Skye were standing above me with a cold rag on my head.

"I think I passed out," I responded.

"No shit, Sherlock," Jayson said.

"Hey, be nice," Skye smacked Jayson on the shoulder. "Help me pick her up and bring her to the car."

Jayson grabbed me and scooped me up. He brought me into the town car and they piled in behind me. I was finally able to sit up on the seat. I needed to get to the airport. First, I needed some water, but then I needed to grab my stuff and go to the airport. I had to get on the next plane to Texas. I looked over to the clock and realized it was already one AM.

I had to meet Rita one last time before the fall really began to pick up, but the airport was more important right now. I reminded myself to call Rita when I got to Texas and explain what was going on.

"Airport. Water," I managed to croak out at Skye.

"What are you talking about, woman? You're acting all kinds of crazy right now. First you pass out, and now you're talking about watering the airport?" Jayson exclaimed.

"No. I need water," I said, while Skye opened a bottle and handed it to me. The cool liquid felt as good as gold as it rushed down my throat and I was finally able to swallow normally.

"I need to go to the airport, so drop me off at home so I can grab my stuff and go," I explained when I was finally able to speak.

"What are you talking about? You're being nuts, Harper Mae," Skye declared as she shook her head, not knowing how to react in this kind of a situation.

"I need to go see him, Skye. I need to touch him and tell him everything will be okay. I need to go make sure we are okay. I don't want to lose him before I even get the chance to show him who I am," I cried desperately, knowing that if he was there with Kylee, I would lose the chance to ever love him again. Everything we had would be over in a matter of a few months, and I couldn't live with that. I needed to know he was there for me and not with other women.

"Okay, okay, crazy lady, hold your horses," Skye said, as she told the driver my address and we pulled out.

"Where did Nate go?" I asked, and saw Jayson shift his eyes uncomfortably.

After a few moments, he said, "He left when you passed out. I think it freaked him out or something, but he said to call when you're feeling better."

"Mm-hm," was all I could manage to respond.

That is the very reason I love Ryder, because even at my lowest points, he would love me. He would never leave me if I had passed out. In fact, he would be so concerned with what was going on he would take over, instead of leaving it up to my friends to do.

It was so late at night, or rather, early in the morning, that I felt exhaustion try to creep over me, but adrenaline kept coursing through my body and I couldn't find the time to rest my eyes.

When we pulled up to my apartment, I leapt out of the car and bound into the apartment, throwing a bunch of clothes into a bag. I called a hotel in Sugar Land and booked a room for a couple of nights. I grabbed one of my coral dresses that would be appropriate to crash a wedding in. I was just hoping he would be there with me and not with *her*. I knew they were going to be there together, but I prayed that I wouldn't actually see Kylee with him. I needed to hold Ryder, and for him to tell me everything would be okay. I needed to feel him inside of me, then everything would make sense.

I ran outside with my bag in tow, and jumped back into the car where Jayson and Skye were violently making out. I coughed a little to get their attention, and Jayson immediately removed his hand from Skye's inner thigh as she started readjusting her skirt.

"You guys, I can just get a cab or something," I offered, knowing they probably wanted some private time.

"No, we are taking you. Don't be a silly goose," Skye said, and she told the driver we were off to the airport.

I picked up the phone and started calling one of the airline companies, trying to get a last minute ticket. As I was giving the representative my information, she interrupted to tell me that I already had a ticket on standby. I could apply it to any flight I wanted. Knowing that the flight was about to cost me hundreds of dollars, a feeling of appreciation swelled inside me. This was what Ryder had meant when he said a ticket would be waiting for me. I booked the next flight, which wouldn't leave until six. Looked like I'd be sleeping at the airport for the next couple of hours. I needed to see Ryder now. I felt anxious and twitchy about having to just wait around; I even toyed with the idea of driving to Texas, but it would take me much longer than if I just waited until 6am for the plane.

When we arrived at the airport, the driver pulled up to the terminal and I grabbed my bag before hopping out of the front seat.

"Please be safe, I love you," Skye said, while giving me a kiss on the cheek.

"He does love you. I know you are going there to try to prove something, but he does love you so much; just remember that, please. Oh, and call Rita!" Skye continued.

"I will, I swear." I hugged her tightly.

"She's right, Harper. He's crazy about you," Jayson said before I left the car. I waved at both of them and hopped out.

I walked inside the airport and suddenly felt my entire body breakdown. I was getting really shaky and anxious. It was probably a mix of passing out, the alcohol, and not eating that was doing me in.

I quickly checked in and grabbed a bite to eat at the small airport Starbucks, before sitting down to wait for my flight.

Once seated at my gate, I plugged in my earphones and played the best music I could find. Everything was going to be okay. I would see Ryder and we both would agree everything was fine. Rest assured, we were going to find each other and everything would fall into place around us. Only distance could keep us apart, but our love was strong enough to withstand the pain of both our pasts.

Chapter 9

Ryder

I checked my phone when I got up to see if Harper had decided to text me back. She hadn't texted, and I felt so fuckin' bad for pissing her off like this. I tried calling again, but no one picked up. Suddenly, there was a loud knock at the door, and I heard Kayden's voice bellow from the other side.

"Get up. We are checking our khakis for the wedding. Meet downstairs in ten," Kayden yelled.

"Got it. I'm coming." I laid my phone back on the nightstand and pulled on my sweats to go downstairs. I gave a big kiss to Evelyn before heading to the dude-side of the house, where the guys were gettin' ready for the big day.

"What's wrong? You're in a funk this mornin'," Kayden finally asked, after I had been given my custom groomsman khakis and shirts with leather cowboy boots.

"Nothing. It's your big day," I replied, not wanting to get into it on his wedding day for Christ's sake.

"Talk to me," Kayden said, and handed me a Redbull.

"It's Harper. She hasn't returned any of my phone calls. I was hoping she would've just come out here, but I think she's still pissed at me. The other night, Kylee slept in my room, and I was too drunk to notice. I thought honesty was the best policy and all that shit, but I guess I would've been better off keepin' that minor detail to myself," I confessed.

"Well, shit. I don't know what to say. Yeah, I have had my fair share of messing up, but when you love someone, you prove it to them no matter what. Looks like you got a lot of suckin' up to do, bro. Maybe call her and just tell her flat out that nothing happened. You talked with Kylee and let her know her bullshit schemes ain't gonna work. You're in love with Harper, and that's not going to change. Just grovel at Harper's feet, and do whatever you can to get her here; if she refuses, then drag your ass onto a plane, and go to her. Just don't give up if you really love her," he answered.

"I know she's the one, Kayden. I know it sounds fuckin' crazy and all, but I know she is the one for me. She just fits perfectly into my life. I mean, I care about Kylee, but she just doesn't fit. I love and respect her as a mother, but she's not the woman for me."

"That's how I felt about Savannah. I just knew. She'll forgive you eventually, Ryder. When you have found the one, you just gotta work hard at 'em. Women are tough to crack, but once you got 'em open, its all smooth sailin' from there. I also have mad amounts of respect for you to be able to take care of a kid when you were so young. I understand where you're coming from," he slapped me on the shoulder and walked away as the tailor called him over.

The rest of the morning was spent getting our clothes perfected, drinkin' a few beers, and preparin' for his nuptials.

***

Savannah had done a great job of plannin' the wedding, because everything was organized down to the very last flower petal. Kylee and I were going to walk down as the third couple, arm-in-arm. Evelyn was the flower girl, who walked behind us. She was beautiful, and I realized I might have to pull out my shotgun sooner than I had expected to ward those boys off.

Kylee looked gorgeous and was made up to look natural, which was a better look than when she tried to put a shit-ton of make-up on her face. She was wearing boots and a dress to match the rest of the bridesmaids.

"Ryder," she said, while taking my arm into hers. I linked with her and we walked down the aisle to the wedding march.

After the long-ass ceremony, we all walked to the barn where the cocktail hour and reception were going to be. The wedding was at Sugarland. We popped a couple bottles and the champagne started flowin'. I was sick of all the pussy stuff, so I grabbed a bottle of Jack and started pouring a glass.

"Whoa there, cowboy," Kylee said, while clinking her glass with mine. She winked, and I knew she was jokin' rather than flirting when she started chuggin' her glass of champagne and gestured for some Jack.

I was shocked at what a different person she could become overnight. Ever since we talked at the diner and made very clear she was nothin' more to me than the mother of our child, she backed off completely. I had a suspicion it's because of the guy she was talkin' about datin'. Fuck it; I was just happy she was finally movin' on. Now she could begin to feel for him what I do for Harper. She looked…happy. It's a look I haven't seen on her in a while. Of course I care for her. She's been my friend since we were kids, and gave me someone I consider one of my greatest loves in life: Evelyn. I did feel a pang of regret for treating Kylee like shit and cheating on her all the time. It was a God-awful time for me, and I needed an outlet for the shit storm that had become my life. I'd fucked many women back then, but had never loved a woman until I met Harper. My Harper.

Maybe everything would work out in the end. Pops and I didn't resolve shit, but I was able to get everything off my chest that I needed to. I had to tell Mom and Pops that they were shitty, neglectful parents who raised me only in the eye of the public; but in the privacy of our own home, I was raised by our housekeeper. A weight was lifted off my shoulders, and I could be the man Harper needed now. If only she was here, I could give her the world on a silver platter. I wanted to make sure she had everything in life. I wanted to spend the rest of my life with her and make her mine. Only a few short hours left in Texas, and then tomorrow, I would go back and take her into my arms.

When we walked to the reception area, we could see the giant white tent that had been set up on the lawn in front of is expansive mansion. We all took turns stepping out of the stretched car and made our way into the extravagantly decorated, outdoor reception. There were some girly, fruity cocktails at the bar, but I could tell Knox had some say in the booze that was served, because there was a cooler full of beer and some kegs for the guys. Thank fuckin' God there was beer, otherwise, my masculinity would be taken away completely. Dinner was a fancy, five-course meal, and the wait between plates was pissing me off. But I calmed down when I saw it was a bad-ass steak, grilled to perfection.

After the dinner was served, the bride and groom did their toasts when the rest of the family and important people said some teary-eyed stuff. Then, the dancin' began, and immediately the entire vibe of the wedding day changed. It stopped bein' boring and annoyin', and there was some excitement and hell to be raised with all our friends around. The guys started twerkin' on the dance floor, which was fuckin' hilarious since most of Knox's friends are all cowboys and have no idea what "twerk" even means. The girls were shakin' their asses, and everyone was gettin' along while the liquor was flowin'. I went to go sit back down at the table to grab some more beer, when someone came over.

The photographer was at our table and wanted to get a photo with me, Kylee, and Evelyn. I went over to call Kylee and Evie in from the dance floor. Evelyn was hysterically laughing from her momma spinning her around. Damn, moments like this made me wish that my parents and I could see eye-to-eye instead of the disasterous relationship we had. I wish I could share this joy without lookin' like a damn pussy too, cryin' and shit.

I went over and ignored the photographer; I started dancing with Evelyn, taking her small hands into mine, and twirling her around. Kylee came over, and we each grabbed ahold of one of Evelyn's little hands, and spun her around as she giggled.

"Momma! Daddy!" she exclaimed loudly.

At this moment, we were in our own little world together. I caught a glimpse of Kylee in between spins, and she was smiling at me. It was nice to see her smile, and to see her genuinely enjoying herself. Her beauty belonged to someone else, and I was happy someone was able to treat her how I couldn't. I was thrilled she could possibly find her version of what Harper meant to me.

The DJ changed the song, and a slow song started streaming through the speakers. Instantly, I picked Evelyn up and started marching around with her, occasionally dipping her. Kylee came up to us and I wrapped my arm around her so Evelyn was squished in between us. We started dancing around each other, holding on so that Evie didn't slip through. We were waltzing around, steppin' on each other's toes, but enjoyin' every moment. We would stop, laugh, and then continue all over again, entertaining Evie until our bellies were sore from our laughter. It was a serene moment we shared with each other, and for the first time in a long time, I felt like I had my family there. Sure, it was a broken family, but I had my daughter there with me and the only thing missing was the other woman I shared my heart with.

"Smile!" I heard the photographer bellow. I almost forgot the fucker was still there. I looked over and propped Evelyn up on my shoulders, and gave Kylee a small peck on her forehead. A moment we could share with Evelyn when she's older, so she could see her parents together and happy. She didn't have to see her parents as bickering assholes like I saw mine. I barely touched my lips to Kylee's forehead when I heard the click of the camera go off. I turned to face the photographer, and that's the moment I saw ***her*** standing there.

It was like the world stopped spinning on its axis, and time stood still. The music in the background faded as I saw her face fall. Harper saw Kylee and me share a small intimate family moment, and I had a damn good idea what she was thinkin'. I knew I had completely fucked up and she was seconds away from bounding out of this place. She misconstrued the whole fuckin' thing.

I'm sure she was racking her brain tryin' to figure out what's goin' on, but it wasn't what she thought.

Shit.

Just, fuckin' shit, right now.

"Harper!" I hollered out, hoping she would hear me through the crowd. Quickly, I turned around and handed Evie back to Kylee, who nodded in the direction of Harper. Almost as if she recognized the shit that was about to go down.

Everything was moving in fuckin' slow motion as I pulled away from Kylee and raced towards Harper. Her face dropped, and she was white as a ghost.

"No," she cried as I reached her. She took her shoes off and started runnin' towards the exit, pushin' her way through the crowded dance floor.

"HARPER!" I yelled, as her head turned around and saw me racin' after her.

I finally caught up to her as she stood on the corner outside, frantically trying to hail a cab.

"Don't even talk to me, Ryder. I have nothing to say to you," she cried, mascara runnin' down her face, and those once-rosy cheeks of hers streaked black.

"Please, Harper, let me explain."

She turned on her heel and looked back at me.

"You are just standing there and watching my heart break a little bit more every second something else comes out of your mouth." I stood there stunned as she hopped in the cab and sped off.

Immediately, I ran to the car Kayden loaned me and followed her.

Chapter 10

Harper

I couldn't believe what I saw could possibly be true. My heart was jumping inside of my chest, and my breath was rushing out of me hard. It felt like I couldn't pick up my feet, but somehow, I flew across the lawn. Inside my head I felt numb and like I was running through quicksand. I needed to feel something. I needed to breathe.

I jumped in the first cab as Ryder screamed from behind me. I couldn't understand what he was saying, it felt like words were speeding past me. All I could picture was the sweet, sentimental moment that I just witnessed between Ryder and his family.

His family.

Something I could never be for him, because he already had one. I knew he came here to be with…her. I couldn't even think her name; it seemed all too unreal.

To some outside person, it looked like a beautiful picture. A photograph of a husband and wife together, with their wonderfully perfect little daughter. To me? It looked as though Ryder was with someone else. It looked as if Ryder came all the way to Houston to deal with his parents, and in turn, found his own perfect, cookie-cutter family. He'd found comfort in the arms of his ex-wife. Just as quickly as he came into my life, he was gone.

He had to go, but I knew he wouldn't. It was up to me to leave. I told the cab driver which hotel I was staying at and gave him an extra twenty, just so he would speed away so Ryder couldn't chase me. I needed him gone quickly. It was like ripping a band-aid off. I knew it needed to be done, but I was so scared of leaving him. Running away was in my blood, but was I really ready to run away from Ryder? I knew he would try so hard to fight for me, but did I want someone who fit so perfectly with someone else?

My logic seemed askew, but sometimes life sends you mixed messages, and it's your job to muddle through them and find an answer.

But I didn't know what to do or who to be. I was scared, frightened that something was just so…different. Ryder was different. I didn't think he would be the type of guy to go after her. I thought he was over her, but I knew when he thought about moving back to Texas with Kylee and Evelyn, that everything we had would just go down the drain.

The cold realization started to sink in. Ryder came down here, and something between him and Kylee rekindled their love for each other. I was going to mean nothing to him, and honestly, he needed his family. I couldn't be that other woman that took him away from all of that. I needed to support him; right now, by supporting him, I had to go. I had to leave him before he sank into this miserable routine, and we ultimately ruined our relationship.

Finally, the cab arrived at the hotel, and I jumped out with tears staining the side of my cheeks. The cab driver was looking at me like I was bat-shit crazy. Hell, I probably was insane, but I needed to go upstairs and call Rita.

Yes, I needed to call Rita. She would have some sort of all-knowing answer, and I wanted to apologize for not coming into work. I paid the driver and rushed inside. I didn't look up, but felt the stares of the front desk staff as I threw myself into the elevator, sobbing uncontrollably.

I pushed the keycard into the room and ran to the bed, flinging myself down on it. My chest was heaving as I curled up against the plush comforter and started bawling. My arms were shaking as I grabbed my cellphone and dialed Rita's number. My hands were heavy as I put the phone to my ear and prayed she picked up. I needed some logic in my life. Everything was so messed up and out of place. I needed someone to tell me not to run, because right now, that's all I wanted to do.

"Hello?" Rita answered in a bored voice.

"Rita?" I sobbed through the phone, my voice laced with pain.

"What's wrong girl?" Her voice perked.

"I don't know what to do. I am so sorry for calling late, but I don't know what to do. I really messed up, Rita," I cried over and over again.

"Girl, don't be apologizing for callin' me. I meant it when I said you can call me anytime. Now tell me what it is that's a botherin' ya?" Rita drawled. "It's Ryder…I just…I can't…" I cried desperately, pressing the phone tightly to my ear.

"What did that boy do?" She asked in a calm and patient voice, waiting for my sobs to slightly subside before she spoke.

"I just came down here for the wedding last minute because I had a nightmare. I just…" The tears rolled down my face like floodgates had been opened.

"Go on, Harper. Tell me what happened to you?" Rita encouraged.

"I just came here to surprise him. I saw him here, kissing his ex-wife with his daughter. I just…I don't know how to take the whole situation," I sobbed.

"Now, what kind of kiss are we talking about, Harper Mae?" Rita asked, her voice was still solid and not worried.

"I mean, it was just on the forehead, but…I just—they were taking a picture together as a family and…" I stopped because Rita quickly interrupted me.

"Girl, are you crazy? Ain't nothing to be worried about. You know, he was probably doing it for his daughter. Trying to get some sort of family picture for her."

"But he came out here for Kylee, his ex. He came out here without me, and initially never invited me out. I know he wants a photo with Evelyn, but damn, did it have to be so intimate? Did he have to kiss Kylee? Was that a necessary thing to do?" I balled into fetal position. I felt naked, vulnerable almost, but the overwhelming feeling to run was taking over my entire body.

"I just want to get off the phone now," I whispered, after sobbing until my throat was sore.

"Now, you listen here. Harper Mae, are ya payin' attention to me right now?" Rita directed. It felt as if she was sitting next to me by the stern nature of her tone.

"Yes," I said.

"Okay, then suck it up and listen up right now. This ain't nothin' to be ashamed of, being upset when you see someone you love in an intimate moment with their ex. Hell, if I saw something like that, I would probably be balling my eyes out too," she said, pausing for effect. "There is something you need to know, though. I keep tellin' you this over and over again, but you aren't seeming to understand me."

"You keep runnin' away whenever you have a problem surface. You keep escapin' until you feel numb to the pain. That numbness you're feeling, it ain't really numbness. It's a disguise for the true feelings. You run because you're scared shitless of facing your problems. Ryder is the one safe thing you got, girl. Go and listen to him at least. Look him in the eyes and see where it takes you from there. Tell him what you are feelin'. Tell him how seein' him with Kylee in that moment irritated you. Tell him you understand that his intentions were good, but that his timin' sucked."

"I don't think I can, Rita. I don't think I can do this anymore. I feel so…deflated and empty. In fact, I don't feel much of anything right now," I confessed, my voice barely above a whisper.

"It's just this moment, Harper. I'm mad you ran off to Texas without showing up to work, but I guess I'll forgive you," she laughed, letting me know she was joking and not serious at all.

"I am so sorry, Rita. I didn't mean to. I just thought coming out here and surprising him would patch things up. Things were rocky before this started."

"What happened?" Rita questioned curiously.

"He was just talking about moving back to Houston…permanently. Something about Kylee wanting to move out here—and of course he needs to be near his daughter. It was just really stressful."

"What stressed you out? You know that boy is crazy about you and would do absolutely anything for you."

"I don't know about that, Rita. I don't think he would. I think he finally realized how over this really is. How I am sort of done fighting for him. There is only so much I can handle; and dealing with his ex vying for him is not something I can handle."

"You can handle anything that is put in your way. I know that for a fact. Now, it's just whether or not you are able to accept that. And that, will determine how you approach this situation."

"I don't know, Rita. I think it's just…over. I think I am just done with the whole thing. I can't be with a man who I am constantly going to wonder whether he is thinking about me, or his ex-wife. I can't imagine a healthy relationship being like that. I have to protect my heart."

"Darlin', your heart is already far away from your chest. It's been gone with Ryder for a long time now. You have an old soul, Harper. You shouldn't be givin' up. Either way, girl, you ain't gonna be doing much listenin' to me. Sounds like you've already made up your mind. But, this is somethin' you'll have to learn on your own."

"I know," I sighed, but surprisingly, the tears started to lessen, and I felt more at peace with my decision. I knew Rita was right, but I had to do what was best for me. I needed to leave before Ryder could hurt me anymore than he already had.

"Thank you for talking to me, Rita. I really needed to hear from you. I am sorry I didn't call you earlier about not being able to show up for work."

"It's okay, Harper. Don't you worry about it. You'll have to just stop by before you get busy with school. And girl, make sure you listen to him. I ain't saying nothin' else, but just listen to him," Rita said before saying our goodbyes and clicking off the phone.

She had a point, I think I just needed to hear him out, but I wasn't sure how to, or what I was even supposed to say to him. Honestly, looking at him right now would make me feel like my world was going to crumble again. All I could think about was that seemingly-innocent kiss with Kylee, and the fact I had the worst timing in the world. How did I manage to walk into the reception at that exact same moment? I would have done anything to go back in time and walked in a few moments later. I didn't want to see him kissing her, but what has been seen cannot be unseen.

It was just so much easier to run than it was to face the problems of reality. Quite honestly, there was a comfort in the idea of running away. Hell, it was what I was good at; running away when shit just started to bounce off the walls was kind of my thing. When I was overwhelmed or stressed, I just ran. I ran away from Tye and his abuse because I didn't know how else to deal with it.

In fact, now that I think about it, Ryder and I are very much alike. He was running away from his past and his family. He hadn't been back to Houston until now, and he was only here because his buddy was getting married. He was constantly in a state of never facing his problems. He was....very much like me.

Shit.

I just couldn't. Two people who are so much alike, who have an incredible amount of baggage, cannot possibly reach their happily ever after, can they? I mean, it seems completely illogical. The kind of love you read in books, see in movies, see in those cute older couples who still hold hands—my pessimistic side said that kind of love doesn't exist anymore.

Therefore, there was no point in being with a man who was *trying* to be with you. Ryder was trying not to think about Kylee. He was consciously making an effort to be with me and not think about her, and honestly, I wasn't one to step on anyone's toes. If he wanted his family whole and complete, who was I to sit here and stop it from happening? It just wasn't right for me to be in the way. I didn't want to be the other woman. I wanted to be his woman, but if that wasn't possible, I would rather see him happy with her, than to be happy myself.

When I started to finally calm down and make peace with the decision, I knew what I ultimately had to do. I slowly peeled off my dress, and stuck my embarrassing flannel pajamas on. I slid under the covers, and clutched the plush hotel pillow tightly against my chest.

This was the best decision I could make…

I thought.

***

The rush of emotions were leaking into my system; and my breathing was hard, but it slowed as I pressed my eyes tightly shut. My arms began to shake violently against my sides; and even though I worked to control my breathing, it felt like my heart was leaping out of my chest.

The wet stink of my sweat started pouring from my forehead, and as I went to try and wipe it, my arms felt forced down by my sides. I needed to wake up, but my brain wasn't having any of that. I tried shutting my eyes and opening them again, but nothing was happening. I was trying desperately to claw my way out of the sheets, but I couldn't. I was forced down, deep into the sinking bed.

"Help me," I tried peeping out, but I found myself in a dark place.

Everything around me was black; even the walls were covered with black. It was a small room, no bigger than a bathroom, but it was completely empty. There was nothing in there except me. Everything was closing in around me, and the walls felt as if they were moving closer and closer.

Suddenly, a loud noise rattled me from my fear and I tried to find out where it was coming from, but there was no one in the room. I was lost in the abyss of my own soul. I tried pawing at the walls, but nothing was coming from it.

How did I become so trapped? Shit. I needed to get out of here, so I tried to close my eyes and opened them again, but still, nothing happened. I was still sitting there in the dark room, so I curled up in one of the corners, hoping this nightmare would end soon.

As the loud noise came again, I was rattled from my shaking desperation. Suddenly, as if someone was writing on a chalkboard, words appeared in white on the pitch black walls.

"SLUT."

"RUNNER."

"ALONE."

"ALWAYS THE MISTRESS."

These words appeared sporadically on the dark wall, and immediately, I began freaking out. Where was this all coming from?! Who was saying these things?

"Who are you? What is this?" I cried, hoping that someone would answer.

Instead, I heard a dark, low rumble of laughter that seemed as though it was coming from the wall. The words stopped, and again, I was consumed by the silence of my past. What was going on? I was confused and dizzy. My mind was spinning in a hundred different directions.

Who was trying to tell me this? Was I dreaming? Where was I? Why wouldn't anyone answer my damn questions? I was desperate for knowledge. Shit, even Tye appearing in this place would provide me some sort of comfort.

I sat in the corner for a few moments with my hands over my ears for fear the penetrating voice would come back and haunt me. When it didn't, I got up to explore the small, closet-sized room.

It was full of nothingness. It was dark, dreary, and bleak. The walls were painted black, and the floor felt like cold tile underneath my feet. It was a room full of painful reminders of the past. The booming voice was nothing but a trace of who I used to be.

"Are you comfortable yet?" The voice echoed again, and I patted the walls to figure out where it was coming from. I didn't see a speaker, or even a small hole in the wall that could have a hidden a microphone in it.

"What do you want?" I cried, hoping that the owner of the mysterious voice would answer, and I could finally escape the numb feeling that was permeating through my body.

"Please," I begged, "tell me what you want, so I can get out of here."

It was quiet for a moment, and again, I was left to ruminate in the thoughts in my head. Breathe, Harper. Just take a big deep breath and breathe.

"You will always be that other woman, Harper. You are useless. A waste of space in the world. Ryder will never love you because you can't love yourself."

"What are you talking about? How do you know me? How do you know that I don't love myself? That could very well not be true," I huffed.

Damnit, look at me. I was sitting here huffing and yelling at a damn wall in a freaking dream. I swear I needed to check myself into an institution, because crazy was taking over my body.

"HA. HA." The voice started cackling like an evil witch from a Disney movie. "Harper, you are nothing to Ryder. He will always choose his family before you. Can't you see that, little girl? He didn't even initially tell you he was coming out here, but he did anyways."

What was this…thing talking about?

I paused for a moment, thinking briefly. This thing could have a valid point right now. Ryder initially didn't even tell me he was coming out to Texas. In fact, he lied to me and didn't tell me anything at all. I had to find out on my own, and he didn't think about inviting me. Was it because he was hiding something all along? Was it his plan to hook up with Kylee and fall back in love with his hometown?

"What if you're right?" God, I really was losing it now. I was trying to reason with a voice in the wall, but I wanted to hear what this thing had to say.

"The truth of the matter is that you will always be the other woman to Ryder. You will always be that woman back in California, but Kylee will be that woman from home. Do you see how that sounds? You will *always* be the other woman, Harper. A mistress. A slut. Nothing but a waste of space."

"No, this cant be true. It simply can't." I crawled to the corner, sitting and clenched my knees tightly to my chest, heaving in slow breaths. I tried pounding the side of my forehead to wake up. I even picked up the skin around my eyelids to attempt to snap out of this dream.

The harsh reality of all of this was that it was true. I would always be that other woman for Ryder, and nothing more. It was time to face the facts. No matter how hard I tried, or how badly I wanted this, it would never happen. I would never be the woman for Ryder.

I wasn't going to be the one to remind him of his home, his childhood, his life, and the biggest one—his daughter. He was always going to have that intimate connection with Kylee that I would never be able to achieve. While I was okay with it, it still secretly stung.

Part of it was jealously. I was jealous that I wouldn't be able to experience that intimate family moment between Evelyn, Ryder, and myself. The fact that I entertained these ideas was obnoxious and juvenile, but love wasn't going to be the bond that kept us together. It was going to take so much work and effort to even surmise being with Ryder.

I was weak, insecure, and vulnerable. I wanted something comfortable and easy. It was completely ridiculous to think that could happen with Ryder. Nothing was ever easy with Ryder; it was always going to be difficult and frustrating. Between Ryder's past and mine, nothing was ever going to be the same between us.

When the voice spoke up again, it's tone changed, and was much gentler and more solemn than earlier. "There is nothing else you can do, Harper. You have to leave him before you end up in the same pattern of running. One word of advice..." There was a dramatic pause for effect.

"When you love somebody, it's supposed to be easy. You know something is wrong when your relationship becomes hard work."

With that, the room was lit, and I was sitting in what appeared to be a normal bathroom. There were white walls, a toilet, a shower, and white tiled floors. I was digesting what the mysterious thing said to me, when tears flowed down my face.

When the stream of tears hit the floor, instead of just disappearing, they turned blood-red. As more tears appeared, more blood pooled beneath me.

Why? How was this happening to me? I needed to run away. I needed to go—make this whole thing stop—but I didn't know how.

I got up and treaded through the redness of the floor, marking up my legs with bloodstains. I pounded on the door, which started to turn red, itself.

"HELP ME! GET ME OUT OF HERE!" I screamed, as I continued to cry, and the blood on the floor continued to pool.

As the growing ocean of red increased, I was suddenly covered head to toe with the stains. All I wanted was to make this stop. All of this to stop.

I wanted Ryder out of my life because he was too hard, too complicated, and brought too many memories out from within me. I was struggling with making all of this work, and it was just so much easier without him in my life. These nightmares scared the shit out of me.

I wanted out.

I needed out.

***

My hands were pulsing under me as I searched for the blood-red stains of the bathroom. I was shaking, as if I was having a seizure and my body was in a state of cold shock. I patted the bed around me, hesitant to find out where I was or who surrounded me.

When I realized there was no blood around me, and I wasn't in a bathroom, I popped my head up to survey the room. The covers were kicked into a pile at the edge of the bed, and the pillows messed up around the sides of the bed.

Holy crap. What just happened to me? Where was I, and what sort of message was trying to be conveyed? Confusion was pounding against my head and I couldn't wrap my thoughts around what that strange unconscious voice was saying in my dream.

Was I really always going to be that other woman to Ryder? Was I too stupid to realize this before we got involved? I mean, seriously, how had I not seen this coming? Of course he was always going to be with Kylee. She was a part of his family because she was the mother of his child. While I loved him with every fiber of my being, I would never be good enough for him. I was always going to be that other woman.

If not literally, then I would figuratively be stuck in that mistress role. If he wasn't going to be with Kylee romantically, I would still always come second and be that other person to him, because he would have to put her first. Truthfully, I wasn't prepared for that. Tye put me second in our relationship, and I didn't deserve to be there. I wasn't prepared to put myself second, and I didn't deserve to have to be put in that position. I was a first-pace kind of gal. Damnit, I should have been treated like a princess, if not a queen.

I guess I was sort of having a moment of what growing up felt like. Intrinsically, I knew I had to move on, and regardless of what my heart was telling me about Ryder, I knew my brain was right in this situation. If this had happened before, when I was still with Tye, I would have let him convince me that everything was actually okay. I would probably have gone back to him, clinging desperately for some sort of emotional connection that I craved.

But this wasn't me back then, this was the here and now. I didn't want to be that girl who goes crawling back to their significant other because they crave the closeness and comfort and that's it. I didn't want to be in a relationship with someone just because it's convenient, or just because its there. I wanted to be in a relationship with someone who would make me his everything. I deserved that, didn't I? After all the shit I had to put up with over so many years with Tye, I knew I fucking deserved it.

Ryder couldn't be that person for me. There just couldn't be a possible way for us to be together without everything becoming so complicated and hectic. Our little life we thought we created a few months ago was nothing but a façade, a fake, bullshit love story you read in books, and not real life. This is real life. This is heartache.

I turned over and picked up the covers, and did my best to fluff them and straighten up. I noticed my phone had dropped to the floor. Instinctively, I picked it up and turned it on. There were over thirty missed calls, and a dozen texts, all from Ryder.

"Baby, you saw something that didn't mean anything."
"Harper, please pick up the phone I am begging you."
"I am coming to see you."
"Don't do this, Harper. Don't run away."

It was almost as if he read my mind. He knew what was running through my thoughts, but I couldn't let him manipulate me into thinking everything was okay. I grabbed my bag and started to gather my things.

I was getting ready to leave when I heard knocking on the door. I walked over and looked through the peephole, which was black.

"Who is it?" I called out.

"Room Service," a low male voice responded.

What the heck? I swear I didn't order any room service. Maybe I did when I was locked in my crazy, subconscious dream world. I carefully peeled the security lock from the door and cracked it open just a tad.

I was quickly thrown back as Ryder busted through and into the small hotel room; sweat was beading on his brow. The rage that burned in his normally cool blue eyes was frightening. His brows were furrowed inward, which showed some of the wrinkles on his forehead. His lips were pursed in a pout, which was so incredibly sexy in a sad sort of way. It took me a moment to react to what was happening, but I felt two strong hands on my wrists. I pulled away and looked at Ryder. His cheeks glistened with a mixture of sweat and tears.

"Harper Mae." He sighed breathlessly.

"How the heck did you find me?" I asked curiously, with a slight undertone of bitch laced in my voice.

"I paid the guy at the front desk to tell me your room number. When you left at the wedding, I followed you. I couldn't let you leave. I could never just let you leave me, Harper," he responded.

"That's kind of creepy, Ryder." I said nonchalantly, and pulled away from him as if I was completely uninterested in what he was saying.

I had to get away from him before I let him convince me that everything was going to be okay. I kept thinking of the dream, and what that weird voice was telling me. I was always going to be that second woman for Ryder, and nothing more. Always a mistress, never more.

"What are you doing here, Ryder?" I hissed at him, this time, annoyed that he was even here pretending like fighting for this was going to work.

"Harper, please stop and let me in." He cried desperately.

"You're in the room; what else could you fucking want?" I bitched.

"I need to explain what you saw. I need to tell you that everything is okay. What you saw isn't what you think it was."

"I know what I saw, Ryder. I saw you kissing Kylee. I saw you sharing an intimate moment with your ex-wife, and that's enough to see. I don't need to see anymore than that."

"But that's not what happened!" He cried, with tears now being angrily swiped away.

Shit, he almost looked sad and desperate. I almost felt like I needed to go to him. I wanted to hold his trembling body in my arms, and rub my fingers through his dark hair. I wanted desperately to tell him that everything was going to be okay with us. Until I realized it wasn't going to be okay with us. Nobody was perfect, but our love is to blame. I relied on him. I depended on him to be there for me, but he wasn't. All I could see was the fact that he was there for Kylee, and not me.

It all started from the very beginning. He was always there for his family, which he should have been, but the least he could have done was talk to me about it all. When he left me at the hotel room when we first met, he should have told me where he was going. It was the first time he took me out on a date, and he abandoned me. He left me there, stuck in the dark, and he was leaving again. This was no different than when we first met.

"It is what happened, Ryder. You left for Texas, the very bane of your existence, without telling me or giving me any clue as to what you were doing. You left me anyways. You are always leaving me. Really, it's what you're good at."

"But— " He tried to interrupt me, but I placed my index finger to his lips to quiet him.

"There is going to be no buts, Ryder. Let me finish, please."

"Go on." He beckoned, frustrated because I clearly wasn't going to let him continue with whatever long-winded speech he had planned on his way here.

"You came out here after telling me repeatedly how hard it would have been to come back to Texas, and didn't tell me you were even planning on coming out here. I couldn't be here to support you, which upset me. Of course I wanted to be out here, but when you brought it up, you told me to stay in California. I would have come on the first plane out if you asked me, but you never even asked. It hurt me." Tears spilled from my eyes, and I turned my face away with wet pain. A pain that was very familiar to me. A pain that told me to leave. It was time.

"Baby…" He tried to walk over to me, but I pushed him away, and he understood and sat back down.

"It didn't end there, Ryder. I wish it ended at the fact that you were just coming out here that upset me. The fact of the matter is that the minute you got here, you ended up sleeping with your ex-wife." He looked defensive, as if he was going to say something about that, but I cut him off quickly.

"I know it was just in the same bed and nothing happened, but do you realize how horribly wrong that is? Do you realize that regardless if you had sex with her or not, how much you cracked my heart in two when you called me to tell me that? It absolutely broke me, so I got on a plane here. I got on a plane to surprise you, and well, quite frankly, we know how that turned out. I was the one surprised."

"I get that you have a daughter, Ryder. I understand that you will always put her first; and I also know that I won't know that feeling until I have children myself. That doesn't mean that you have to have that same emotional connection with your ex-wife. I know that much. I am a naturally jealous person, and that's just a flaw that I know I have. I could work on it, but I think anyone would be disgusted with your behavior."

"I know, Harper. It was wrong of me. I'm totally aware of it. But, please…don't leave me," he begged, as he grabbed my wrist.

I shook him off and continued, "Then I come here, so excited that I was finally going to be able to surprise you, and what do I see?!" I screamed at him.

"I see you with your stupid ex-wife, holding each other, and you are kissing her on the forehead. You KNOW how much I love that, right? You know how I thought it was our special thing—to kiss each other on the forehead. It was such a 'fuck-you' to our relationship. You sharing our special moment with another woman."

"Harper, that's not how…"

I couldn't let him continue. I was heated, and anger was coursing through my veins. It felt almost like there was a large gaping hole in my soul and he kept prodding it with a knife.

"No. FUCK YOU, Ryder!" That pretty much summed up how I felt. There wasn't really much more I could say or do. I wanted him out of this tiny little hotel room. But, I continued my word-vomit assault, all while watching his face morph through a range of different emotions. I wanted nothing to do with this piece of shit.

He shared *our* personal and private moments with other people, and I was getting so fucking sick of his shit. I was sick of having to share myself with the world. When I was with Tye, I was shared with the abuse I had to encounter. I was sick of sharing myself with pasts.

I had worked very hard to not share myself with Ryder, but he was still sharing me with Kylee. I felt like I had to work to steal him from his past, and I wasn't sure if I had the gusto in me to continue fighting for him. Essentially, his past was going to win and take him away from me.

"Fuck you for going back to your ex-wife. Fuck you for making me confess everything to you and then go stab me in the back…again. Fuck you for having an ex-wife in general, who you can't seem to get away from. Just, seriously, get the fuck out of here, because I can't do this anymore. It's over, and I don't want to do anything else with you. I want nothing to do with you anymore. I have to leave." Tears were spilling down my face now, and my hands were shaking beneath my solid composure.

"Don't say that, Harper! I can't lose you. I don't know where I would be without you. All I wanted to do was come back home to you and tell you everything that happened with my family and this trip. I was stupid and thought I could do all of this without you, but I realized I can't. I cannot live without you. I don't know how to breathe without thinking about you. You are the center of my world. No, you are the center of my universe. I am sorry for hurting you. You know I would never intentionally do anything to hurt you. I just thought…" he wanted to keep going, but I interrupted him.

"You thought nothing. That's the problem, Ryder. You didn't think about shit."

"No, in fact, I was thinking about Evelyn. I thought that when she grows up, she would want one simple picture of her family. A picture of her, her mother, and her father in one frame. That's what I was thinking," he said, as he gently laid his hands on top of mine, which were fidgeting in my lap.

"But you could have easily taken that photo without kissing her on the forehead. You knew how much that gesture meant to me," I cried, desperate for him to know how much that small thing pained me.

"I know it was wrong of me, Harper, but I can't lose you." He dropped down from the bed, and was on his knees in front of me. I looked up from my hands, and glanced at his face. His eyes were red and puffy from crying, and his hair was fluffed all around his face from constantly raking his hands through it. He had slight lines on his lips, which were turned downwards. He looked…sad. Really, that's the only way I could describe his features. He looked pained, as if at any moment I was going to run and never come back…which was true. I was going to leave.

I had to leave.

"I have to go, Ryder. I can't do this to myself anymore. There's just too much pain, and it's just not worth it. I am so used to going back to the person who hurts me the most, but this time, I am trying to be independent and a bigger person. I am looking out for myself for once in my life; and with that, I have to go. I just simply can't."

Ryder got up and started pacing the small hotel room.

"Harper, my life is all about you. And if you just left me, you would rip a small part of my heart out and take it with you." He came over to me after pacing back and forth a few times.

"I just can't, Ryder. It's the timing of all of this. Right now, I just can't do this. You have some issues you need to work through with your past, and I have some shit I have to deal with. The timing between us was always too perfect and too right, but it just fell apart. You have to accept that things might fall apart to come back together." I had hoped that maybe with a light at the end of the tunnel, it would be easier to leave. He needed that hope I was trying to give to him.

"I don't want you to leave, Harper. I want to work through this," he begged, now standing above me.

"I have already worked through it, and it's over. I am done with everything we had. I have to go, and I really don't want to make this any harder than it already is." I secretly hoped it would be easier than this.

I urged that numb feeling to come over my body because I needed it to protect me from the rush of emotions I was actually feeling. I was trying to be strong and make it appear that this was easy for me. It was an easy coping mechanism I used to escape the harsh realities of life itself.

That thing in my dream was right though, and always the voice in the back of my head when I felt like I was going to crack. I had to realize I was always going to be that other woman to Ryder, and no matter what he said, nothing was going to change that. He was never going to change and I knew that. I just had to make the best out of this so we could leave as easily as he came into my life.

"Please, don't do this. Look at me, Harper. I'm broken in two. I'm cryin' like a damn baby right now. I don't want to think about my life without you in it. Who will I wake up with in the mornin'? Who will be curled up next to me when I open my eyes? Who am I going to talk to about my day? Who will sit next to me, eatin' junk food and rubbin' their incredibly sexy body against mine?" He cried, and when he stopped, waterworks came down my face.

It pained my heart because he didn't think I was going to miss all of that too, that I was dreading losing him for those reasons.

"I don't want to do this!" Ryder cried, dropping to his knees.

"It's already done," I whispered.

His hands reached up and grabbed the top of my head; while he rubbed his soft fingers through my hair, I watched the pools of water drip from his eyes. This was going to hurt both of us, but it had to be done. His face was still turned in a gut-wrenching frown, but something else came over his body. It was almost like a hunger to taste me one last time. To share a moment together that we both knew was going to be the last moment of it's kind.

I grabbed his hands and put them back down. I wasn't sure if I was ready for one last time with him. I just sort of wanted a clean break, but this was going to happen. It was a moment that was bound to occur. We were initially bound by our intimate ties, so it made sense that we would be broken by them.

"I'm so sorry," he groveled, while taking my waist and pulling me into his. Tears started forming in his eyes again as he stared at me with his infamous blue eyes, which were a shade darker tonight.

His lips touched mine gently, as if he was yearning for more, but oh-so-careful not to upset me or surprise me. When they touched mine, there was a spark that elicited hope throughout my body, but I quickly suppressed that thought. This was goodbye and nothing more. We both knew it. It was over, what we had was something amazing, but neither of us could do it anymore. When a relationship became too difficult, it was easier just to give up, and I was giving up and letting go.

His hands slowly moved from my sides and ran through my hair, pushing it back while he looked at me, tears now exploring the bottom of his cheeks.

"I will—" he began, when his lips left mine.

"Shh," I commanded, and pressed my lips against his, inhaling his scent and taking him in one last time. I pushed him against the wall, and he grabbed my legs and lifted me up. I wrapped my legs around his waist and crossed my feet so I wouldn't slip.

Emotions were eating at me, and I felt so completely empty and worthless that I hugged him tightly, trying desperately to feel something with him. I was in this for the long haul at one point, but I couldn't believe anything he said now, and the trust we'd had was broken. I saw the look on his face when he talked about having a family with Kylee and Evelyn, and I had to let him go.

"It doesn't have to happen like this, Harper." He whispered hoarsely, desperately hugging me tighter to him and lifting my legs as high as they would go around his hips.

"It has to be like this, Ryder. Me and you? We are just two people who have bad timing and too many secrets to have a healthy relationship now."

I kissed him desperately so he wouldn't respond, and he countered my attack by slipping his velvety tongue into my mouth, caressing me deeply. He walked over to the bed, not letting go with his lips once. He threw me on the plush hotel bed and got on his knees as he pushed me up towards the headboard.

"God, you are beautiful," he groveled, the tears still wet on his cheeks.

He slipped his hands under the hem of my shirt, and I willingly lifted my hands up as he slid the shirt past my arms. His hands moved slowly down my neck, past my shoulders as he circled them slowly around my body. It was almost as if he was trying to memorize the curves of my body. His hand slipped behind me and unhooked my bra with one hand, yanking it off my body. My tits spilled out and his mouth went down immediately to suckle my nipples hard—so hard it almost hurt. His tongue was darting in and out, and his teeth lightly nibbled.

He pressed his lips down my stomach, kissing each area with gentle ease. When he reached the top of my pajama bottoms, he yanked them off, exposing the black thong I was still wearing from the dress I had on at the wedding. He looked down at me, and as the wet tears still dripped onto my naked torso, he smiled and pulled his hand under the lace seam of the underwear.

"Don't even think about it," I dared, as a big *rip* echoed through the room. My underwear was in two pieces as he laughed and threw them on the floor.

His mouth came down on my shaven pussy in a fury, as his tongue desperately circled the outside of my clit, making me yearn for more. The desperation in his tongue to find more and go deeper was evident as the pressure inside of me was pushed further. I needed him, and he understood exactly what to do as his tongue circled the outside of me and he slipped two fingers inside of me, pressing up against the walls of my swollen core.

Everything was different this time as he stared at my mouth contorting with pleasure. It was almost as if he was eager to please and make me happy. He needed to see me climax because he wanted to experience something with me that no one else would ever be able to do.

His mouth moved slowly from me, and he wiped off his lips as he kissed back up to my navel and towards my neck, stopping for a moment to slowly bite my right ear ever so carefully.

His eyes permeated deep into my soul as he stared at me and thrust himself inside of me at the same time. His eyes never faltered as he pushed deeper inside of me, letting me feel the extent of his size. I cried out and arched my back, my head involuntarily falling back.

"No," he demanded, and cradled my head in his hand so that he could see my face.

Everything was different this time around. His movements were slower, and he stared at me as he pushed in and out very gently, taking his time to caress me. His lips descended down onto mine, and he hungrily tried to find the connection between us that we both knew we would lose the minute this ended.

I pushed him up so that he had to pull himself out of me, but quickly had him re-engaged by getting on top of him. Slow tears started tickling the lids of my eyes, but I pushed forward, grinding roughly onto him while moaning with pleasure.

His pain was evident in his face, which was contorted into something I couldn't recognize. This, for us, wasn't anything we had done before. This moment was full of lust, love, passion, but mostly pain. The pain we both felt leaving each other stranded and alone in this heavy world. I leaned deeper into him, calling out from pleasure as he grabbed my tits and pushed hard against them. The bed rocked back and forth as I rode him deeper into a tireless oblivion. I felt every vein of his dick inside of me as I drove further onto him.

"Please," he cried out.

His voice was laced in both sexual desire and loss knowing that this intimate moment we were sharing with each other would be our last. This moment was going to end as quickly as it started. I clung onto him desperately, until he grabbed my hips and picked me up. I wrapped my legs tightly around his back and continued to bounce on his dick, keeping him deep inside of me while he carried me and threw me against the wall.

"Fuck!" I moaned, as he pinned my arms against the unforgiving wall and thrust deep into me, hitting me in my precious g-spot.

My tits felt sore they were bouncing so hard, and I had no control over my hands, so I was writhing in pleasurable pain. We were stuck like this for what seemed like forever, him pounding into me over and over again with such speed and desire that I thought my vagina was actually going to implode at a certain point. It all came to a sudden halt when he stopped abruptly and grabbed onto me, throwing me back onto the bed and leaning close to me.

His lips met mine ever so gently as he caressed them with his. I couldn't hear anything, but felt the wetness on his cheeks, which was clearly tears coming from his eyes. I knew immediately that he had been crying.

"Baby, I am so sorry. You have to forgive me," he cried while still pushing his dick into mine, but this time, there was no intense desire, but rather a gentle ease in which he did so.

Tears started pricking my eyes as well, as we both looked at each other and he pushed deeper inside. I had never had sex like this…if that's what I could even call it. It was something indescribable. I couldn't put my finger on it, but what we shared in that moment was pure, unadulterated, and unfiltered love for each other. There was no one else around us, just the intimate moment between Ryder and myself. For a second, I thought that maybe this could really mend our relationship, and maybe there was a sliver of a chance for us to move forward; but alas, it wasn't true. Sex was going to end, and then it would be back to reality. So, instead, I drove my hips into his, shoving his member into my throbbing core. I ground into him until I felt tension build up inside of me.

"I…am….going…to…" I cried out when I couldn't hold it anymore.

"Cum for me, baby," Ryder moaned, thrusting himself deeper and deeper.

As the pressure built up inside of me, I felt a sudden burst of release as I let go all over Ryder's aching dick. He cried out desperately, as I felt him release his built-up pressure all over me. I felt the warm liquid spill against my stomach as he moaned with inane pleasure. Quickly, I cleaned my stomach off, and began to crawl away from him onto the other side of the bed. He started to crawl next to me, but stopped in the middle of the bed. I pushed him away, not allowing him to get close to me or start to cuddle with me.

Rather, he looked over at me with sadness in his face, but with a knowing glance that everything we once had ended with that orgasm. He slid in next to me, and tucked himself under the covers. "I know you're not going to understand what I am doing, but it hurts. The pain I feel inside of me is as if someone keeps stabbing me over and over again," I whispered to him, as he just continued to sit and stare at me. It was almost as if he was trying to take me in and study my every movement and feature.

"I know, Harper. I understand." He whispered very quietly. We both were silent again, but Ryder continue to glance at me while his eyelids were getting heavy.

He slid next to me and grabbed onto my stomach, pulling my back into his chest and holding me tightly. I let him. I owed it to him, at the very least, to hold me and to feel his warmth against me. I felt the warm, teary sensation come again, and small droplets fell onto the bed, as I understood this was going to be the last I saw of Ryder Andrew Kent. This was going to be the last of an era and a moment in my life. There was going to be no more of this ever again, and I had to just sit back and ride this wave until it crashed against the shore. "Just let me stay here tonight. Just like this, please," he begged me, pushing me further against him. I felt as though I was going to actually connect to his body if he pulled me any tighter.

"Okay," was all I was able to croak out. As the night turned into early morning, I wasn't able to get any sort of sleep, but I could hear Ryder next to me snoring softly in his sleep.

I didn't think I was strong enough to face him in the morning. What were we even going to say to each other? 'Oh, thanks for letting me fuck you, but I have to leave now?' Was he going to try to make me stay with him? There was no way I could even begin to do that. I needed to go. At this point, I had my heart set on going, and knew that if he tried to convince me, I would stay. I was weak and infantile, easily pressured to doing something that I knew was going to fail anyways. Our relationship was over, and while it was wonderful and a complete and utter fairytale while it lasted, not all fairytales get their happy endings. Our ending sucked. Plain and simple.

I quickly and quietly rolled off the bed, glancing over at Ryder to see if my movements had woken him up. He was still sleeping soundly, but curled up in a fetal position. This hurt. Sure, it was my idea and my fault for doing this, and I probably could have worked it all out with Ryder, but I couldn't let myself be that weak again. I couldn't go back into old patterns like I had in the past with Tye. I was a different person, and I had Ryder to thank for that, but I still needed to be me.

The new Harper, who didn't fall into old patterns and let others walk all over her. The new Harper didn't let people skate by her, or did what others said just to please them. No, I was going to take this stand for myself because I had to. There was simply no other way around this. With that, I grabbed my bag, and stuffed everything I had come to Texas with, which wasn't much to start, and clicked away on my phone until I was able to book a plane ticket home.

When I was ready to leave, I glanced over at Ryder one last time. This was it. It really was the last time I was going to see him, laying there so peaceful and satisfied. I couldn't imagine the pain that was going to perpetuate on his face in the morning. It was going to be trying and hard for both of us. It was going to be so fucking excruciating to get over him, but I just had to keep reminding myself that I was doing this all for my sanity. It was all for me. A cacophony of emotions was bubbling from inside of my chest, and an explosion was forthright and imminent. I needed to escape from here, and from him, now. I needed to run away from the pain that was welling in my chest. I grabbed the last of my clothes and stuffed them into my small suitcase, making sure not to make a single peep. That was it. My great, epic romance was over and I was back to square one.

I was clearly a disaster that not even Ryder was able to tame. When my bag was finally packed, I quickly tiptoed outside the room and locked the door behind me. Locking away the pain I couldn't bring myself to bare anymore. He didn't love me, it was clear when I saw him kissing *her* last night. I could never be that family he longed for, and with that, I knew I had to leave. I walked down the long hotel hallway until I clicked G on the elevator.

Everything I was doing felt so methodical and robotic, even when hailing a cab. I was numb to the emotions inside me. It was time to escape. Far away from the pain Ryder had caused me.

Chapter 11

Ryder

I fell asleep lying next to the love of my life, and woke up to an empty bed. I suspected she would leave during the middle of the night, but was tryin' to hope for the best. Damn, it's like missin' something that you didn't even know you had until it left. Stumbling out of bed, I went over to the bathroom to see if maybe she left some of her stuff on the counter, but I didn't see anything.

She was gone. Just with a snap of my fingers, she had disappeared out my life. I felt like such a goddamn pussy crying last night when we were together like that, but shit, it was like she pressed some button inside of me and I didn't know how to switch it off. It was fuckin' pathetic of me, but I knew I fucked up bad when I saw her running out of that wedding reception.

I grabbed whatever clothes were on the floor and left the room in the mess that we created last night, double checkin' to make sure Harper hadn't forgotten anything. The least I could do was send it to her or somethin'…

Fuck. What the hell was I going to do without my woman? It seriously felt like I was missin' a limb without her. I needed her. No, I fuckin' craved her. Honestly, I didn't get it. Maybe I'm too goddamn stupid to even understand her logic in all of this, but I didn't get why she had to go. It just wasn't clicking in my brain.

She was everything to me. To this moment, she's the light of my life; and everything I do, I do with her and Evelyn in mind. Yeah, I fucked up, and I know I fucked up real bad, but that doesn't mean shit in the bigger picture. I fucked up once. We are all human; we are bound to make mistakes, so I'm not sure why she can't forgive me for this.

I bet it's her goddamn pride. I swear, if I could get my hands on that fucking piece of shit Tye from her past, I'd kill him. I would cut his balls out of his sack and shove him as far down his throat. That motherfucker shouldn't even be breathin' and wouldn't be when I was through with him. That little shit fucked up Harper so bad. All our issues in our relationship lead back to that little bastard. Heartless little shit.

I mean, in that sense, I get why she had to leave. She felt like my dumbass had betrayed her. I can't stand being that asshole to her. I fuckin' hate it. She didn't deserve it and I gave it to her. I gave her the same feelin' she felt with Tye, and I couldn't deal with that personally. That is why I had to let her go.

Fuck. Me.

I needed to hail a cab from the hotel to go back to Knox's house. I knew Knox and Savannah had probably already gone away on their honeymoon, and I was due at the airport in a couple hours; but honestly, I wanted to get back to San Diego as fast as I could. This trip was a disaster and I was ready to just be home.

Damnit. Home wouldn't even feel like home anymore. Without Harper there, sitting in the front room and runnin' up to greet me...there was nothing there for me. There wasn't anything for me anywhere.

The only way I could describe this feeling right now is how I felt when my knee was crushed under the tackle in my last professional football game. It was crushing, like every piece of bone in my body was cracking so slowly that I could hear it peel apart down to its core. That same feeling is what my heart was currently doing to itself. Everything in my body was numb except for the ache in my heart.

I was goin' through the motions, but nothing was really working for me. I hailed the cab, told him directions, and we drove off—drove off from what I thought was going to be the last memory I would ever have of Harper Mae.

I'll never forget her sweet little body wrapped around mine while she stared at me with her big, beautiful brown eyes that were pooling with soft tears. While her plump lips were pursed in a gentle O as she slowly slid down onto me. Damn. I felt myself gettin' a hard-on just thinking about her.

Suddenly, though, reality fucking crashed down hard on me when I realized it was never gonna happen again. I would probably never see her again. I started choking up in the cab, but couldn't look like a fuckin' little bitch in front of the driver, so I pretended like I was coughin' up a loogie or some bullshit.

The entire rest of the ride, I just stared outside, watching Texas pass by my window as we got closer to Sugarland. Once we pulled into Kayden's driveway, I tipped the driver, passed the security check and walked into the house. As I suspected, Knox was nowhere to be found, but surprisingly, neither was Kylee or Evelyn. I walked to my room, just about to give Kylee a call to make sure Evie was okay, when I saw a note scribbled on my bed. Once I picked up that note, I realized another one sat by it's side. The first one was from Knox.

Bro,

I don't know what happened to you at the reception. Heard some blubbering story from Kylee and Savannah about how Harper caught y'all makin' out or something. Dude, I heard how you were talkin' about Harper, so don't go fuckin' that up. I'm fuckin' serious. I had to leave early this morning to catch my flight for the horneymoon with my new wife. I'll give you a call back when I get back into the US of A. Maybe, come visit your pad in San Diego.

Go get the girl. Don't let her go.

-KK

If it wasn't gay as hell, I probably would hug Knox and tell him I loved the shit outta him. I could seriously count on him for anything, and I appreciated the hell out of that. He had to need to come down to San Diego to visit when he gets back. I grabbed the other note, which was clearly written by a woman, someone whose handwriting I would always recognize. Kylee.

Ryder,

I know this is going to be hard for you to read, and right now I am the last person you are ever going to want to see, but we need to talk when we get back to San Diego. I know the thought of me sabotaging your relationship has crossed your mind, and before it gets any closer to your thoughts, make it stop, because I swear to you, I never would deliberately do anything like that ever. I am happy in my own blossoming relationship and would never do anything to intentionally harm yours. I promise you that I did, at one point, want more from you, but right now? I want to be a mutual parent with you, and nothing more.

I will love you every day because of the past we have, but I am no longer in love with you. I see the way you speak about Harpe,r and you never talked about me like that. I saw the way you defended yourself to your parents, and that is something you never would have done when we were together. We were just two young kids in love. We were too damn young for our own good, but hey, we got a beautiful little girl from it all.

I know this isn't making any sense right now, but basically, what I am trying to say in this convoluted mess, is to go get the girl. You deserve happiness. No, we both deserve happiness, and I see how happy Harper makes you. I know that by her seeing that kiss, it really upset her, and so I am going to make it a point of mine to go explain to her what happened. I think it will help to see her face to face. You cannot talk me out of this one. I am doing this for you; remember that before you start screaming.

I am taking Evelyn back to San Diego with me. You can come pick her up, not this weekend, but the next. I will text you with more details.

-Kylee

Damnit. I was fumin'. My hands were shaking as I ripped the letter in two. I didn't want Kylee fuckin' this up anymore than she already was with the stupid fuckin' picture I wanted. FUCK. Pissed wasn't even close to describing how I felt. I started grabbin' my shit and throwing it in the suitcase, when suddenly I realized something, like a light bulb clickin' on in my brain.

What could Kylee possibly fuck up even more? Harper wasn't mine. She made that very clear last night and when she left early this morning. She ran away from me, and there was nothing I could do to convince her otherwise. It was over, so why not have Kylee go over and talk to her?

Worst-case scenario is that Harper gets pissed, or doesn't even show up to their meeting. Best-case scenario, it plants a little seed in Harper's brain that maybe she was wrong about this. Because she *is* wrong about this. All of this. There is nowhere else I would rather be than cuddled up with her in our bed, listening to the waves lap on the shore as the sun sets through the window.

That's so lame of me to say, but love had made me a pussy and I don't give a fuck about that. I don't care what others see me as. I don't care if this is supposedly weak and immature of me. I don't care if this makes me less of a man. Because, damnit, I love my woman, and I would do anything to keep her close to me in my life. There will be nothing and no one in the world that would stop me from loving her and holding her tight in my hands.

Fuck it. If it works, I'll let Kylee go and talk to Harper. I ain't fightin' with her about it. I just wanted to get home and fix all this. I wanted to show Harper that I could be the man for her. If it's space she wanted, I would give it to her; but I hope she doesn't think that I am just going to simply move on from her, because that ain't ever gonna happen. Harper Mae is mine, and always will be. I love her with every damn bone in my body.

I needed to get to the airport. I grabbed one of Knox's drivers and told him I was runnin' late. He said that Knox left him here to give me a ride anyways, and he would gladly take me to the airport.

Thank God.

It was time to get home.

Once I got to the airport, though, it felt like it was taking for-fuckin'-ever to get on the damn plane. Between lugging the bags to the security station, then to the next, then waiting for the plane, I was getting antsy. It was my turn to prove to Harper what she meant to me, and I was going to find some way to do that for her. I was going to find the path back to her, because I didn't know what I would do without her.

I boarded the plane and realized that even though it might take just going through the motions of everyday life, I was going to find my way back to her if it killed me.

I was going back home to find the love of my life.

Chapter 12

Harper

It was like I was just going through the motions of everyday life on auto-pilot. There was no living for me. The days all started to mesh together, and everything seemed like a blur once I got into a rhythm and routine of living without Ryder. I was going straight from school to my apartment. I couldn't even call it home anymore because that's not what it felt like. Home still felt like it was with Ryder…

I thought about him…almost every day. Even if I tried not to think about him, he would always permeate the depths of my brain. He was always with me, stuck in my head. I couldn't shake myself of him, even if I wanted to. So, the best type of coping skill I knew how to do was to become numb. I became frozen from all thoughts, and just continued to go through life like others expected of me.

It was like someone was pressing fast forward and I just kept moving. Seconds turned into minutes, which turned into days, and weeks started to pass, and I didn't even know what I was doing. I would go to school during the day, and come home at night to finish some homework. After my work was complete, I would watch some mind-numbing television show about women bickering about their stupid lives, and then go to bed. Rest and Repeat.

This was my life since I got back from Texas. I hadn't spoken to Ryder at all in the last couple weeks either. He tried calling a couple times right when we both got back, but I didn't have it in me to pick up, and he hadn't called since then. I would be lying if I said I was glad he stopped trying. Although the lack of trying just showed me that he doesn't really care. Shit, he probably had already moved on to some second-hand bitch anyways. Hey, whatever floats his boat.

It's just that…I missed him. I really freaking missed him. I didn't expect any of this to happen, and I kept replaying the scene with Kylee in my head. All I wanted to do was get that out of my head, but it keeps scrolling through my memories like a Rolodex.

It's almost as if I was living some sort of nightmare that kept repeating itself. I couldn't go left, couldn't dodge right—instead, I was sitting here stuck in the mud, trying to trudge out of this painful past that I lived in.

Skye had tried to get my attention at school, and even tried to get me talking about the wedding, but I just put on a fake smile and usually something like "wow" or "that's great Skye," came out of my mouth. I just didn't have the strength to say anything else to her, or anyone in general. I had started feeling kind of bad because I knew it's wasn't her fault, but I just didn't feel like doing anything.

When my show was over at night, I undo my bed and curl up in my plush sheets. Usually, I would grab one of my pillows, and that's when the tears just pour out of my eyes. It's like I knew this is my biggest mistake, but I couldn't stop myself from continuing down this path. It felt most nights like the air was being sucked right out of my lungs, and I couldn't breathe.

Some nights, I was uncontrollable. I shook as if I was seizing, and my body couldn't control itself. It let go and it took me a while to compose myself. I looked it up on the internet and it said I was experiencing panic attacks. I thought the mental illnesses ended with Tye and the depression I had then, but clearly I was wrong.

I guess I was wrong about my mental health in general. You can't just "get over" something like others kept telling me. When I was with Tye, everyone kept telling me that it was okay, and that I would eventually get over him—but they were wrong. Society was wrong. When you've had a broken your heart, once you have it under control it doesn't mean everything is "fixed." No, in fact, quite the opposite.

I think it's part of the reason why I had to leave Ryder. I thought that by falling in love with Ryder, he would be able to patch up the problems of my past...but I was wrong. No one else can fix you; you have to fix yourself. It's a lesson I guess I had to learn the hard way. I didn't want to have to rely on Ryder for happiness anyways.

I just thought that maybe Ryder would be by my side as I ventured down the road of self-healing and finding myself, but once he broke that trust, there was no coming back from that. Trust was quintessential in any relationship, and I just felt so burned from him.

In the same sense, I felt conflicted. I wanted him to be here next to me. I wanted to sit and hold his hand and let him kiss me on the forehead goodnight. I wanted to touch him at night.

There were nights when I dreamed of his fingers slowly caressing me. I imagined his fingers skimming the outside of me, making his way inside, but teasing me first. I imagined Ryder there, speaking sweet nothings in my ear, causing me to reach the point where I could get wet all on my own by just imagining the things he whispered.

Oh God, how I craved him pressing his talented wet lips against my sex. His mouth's wetness colliding with my own, as his touch became fierce and aggressive. His fingers slipped inside of me, as I moaned out loud. It was almost as if I could feel him slamming his fingers against the walls inside of me.

I slowly mustered up the courage and slipped my fingers into myself, moaning as I pictured Ryder's blue eyes staring into mine as he pushed himself inside of me, making me wince at the size of him. I pictured his seductive smile slowly forming when he watched himself pleasure me, thrusting deeper inside of me. I pushed my fingers deeper into myself as I moaned, imagining Ryder slipping his tongue across my breasts, then lightly biting my nipples.

Instantly, I felt a rush of cold come over me as I flick quickly against my clit. I use my free hand to lightly touch my naked breasts, and closed my eyes again, picturing Ryder's rock-hard cock slamming into me, forcing me to scream. God damnit…yes!

I imagined him picking me up and throwing me onto the counter in the bathroom, where I propped my legs up and he inserted himself inside of me. He grabbed onto my legs as he pushed roughly into my deepest parts. I imagined him pulling out and bending down to put his wet, warm tongue against me. I groaned as he tasted me from the inside out.

As I pictured him licking me up, I pushed my fingers in farther and squeal as I hit my G-spot. I could feel it there, so I flicked my fingers in a circular motion that sent vibrations all the way up to my belly. The contractions were forceful, and the need to feel more was immanent in my body. The ministrations of my hungry fingers against the walls of my pussy sent me into a fury of excitement. I was quivering, turned on, and raw from the need for release.

I could feel the pressure building inside of me, and suddenly, all I wanted to do was be able to orgasm all over the sheets. So, I closed my eyes, and once again, was greeted by the baby blue pools of Ryder's eyes, and the large, fierce, and hard cock waiting for my wet pussy.

"I have waited for so long, baby," he groaned out, right before he slipped inside of me.

"Fuck. Me. Hard!" I cried out between thrusts.

He slammed inside of me repeatedly, ramming his large cock inside me, toying with my G-spot. I felt myself on the edge of letting go against him, but wanted this to continue, so I pushed through as he grunted louder, slamming against me.

There was a mirror behind us, and I could see him watch himself fuck me; but I didn't want him to have all the pleasure, so I flipped around and imagined watching myself as he inserted himself back into me from behind, grabbing my hips as I pushed against him. I pictured my face as I was getting fucked with pleasure, and contorting in such a way that I felt as if I was going to burst all around him.

I envisioned him making his "about to orgasm" face as he flipped me over once again, and propped me against the sink. Finally, the pressure inside of me that was building with gentle ease, was too much to handle and I looked at him, both of us knowing what the other was thinking.

I pictured wrapping my legs against his hips as he pushed inside of me one last time. I felt my g-spot get rocked, and I released all over his cock, writhing in such pleasure that my body was shaking all over. I imagined him roaring in that same pleasurable tone I just exhaled, and groan as warm liquid poured into my body

Just as I imagined all of this, I felt myself get wet all over my fingers. The release inside of me felt magical. I had never done something like that before. It was all sort of new and exciting for me. I can't tell you how I felt after doing it all to myself, I just felt so empowered.

I got up and went to go just clean myself up a little bit but opted to hop into the shower to calm my body down from the intensity of my orgasm that just shot through my core.

As I got into the cold shower, I thought about how I had never really touched myself…down there before. It was such a freeing and relieving feeling to be able to do that to yourself. It felt as if I didn't have to rely on a man to get pleasure. I could do it all myself without anyone else's help. I felt like a new person.

As I grabbed the shower gel and started rubbing it all over my body, I was excited to realize that it was me who had given myself the relief it needed. Granted, it was brought on by imagining Ryder in my head, but I did it all myself. Just like I was going to get through this breakup. I was going to do it all myself.

Fuck yes. I was going to be that stereotypical independent woman. Fuck Ryder. I didn't need his dick to pleasure me. I could do it myself. I mean, yes, I had to imagine his dick inside of me in order to turn myself on, but that was irrelevant…or was it?

Fuck. It was confusing and annoying to dwell on, so I just tried to put that thought out of my head. Suddenly, while I was in the shower, I heard my phone ring from the nightstand in my room. My heart skipped a beat and I was hoping that maybe it was Ryder, somehow telepathically getting my sexually frustrated vibes. There was just something in my gut that told me to get out of the shower and go check who was calling; so quickly, I washed off the soap and hopped on out.

I threw on a towel and ran to my phone charging on the nightstand. I looked at the screen and shock rushed through my body.

Holy.

Fucking.

Shit.

Why the fuck would this person be calling me? What would they want, or even have to say, to even begin to have the nerve to pick up the phone to call me. What would they even begin to say to make up for the pain they caused, and the relationship that was ruined because of their stupid thoughtless actions?

But I had to admit, I was curious. So I picked up the phone and answered the call…

Chapter 13

Ryder

I tried to let her go. It was hard at first, 'cause I kept finding myself tryin' to call her or touch her at night. But eventually I got the fuckin' picture when she didn't even bother pickin up. It's been just a waste of a goddamn couple of weeks. All I can do is go through the motions of livin', but she is always on my mind. She haunts my every thought. I would do anything to have my Harper Mae back in my arms.

How the hell do I know she's not out there fuckin' other guys already? It made me disgusted to think that some sick fuck would be tryin' to hit on *MY* woman. And the fact I couldn't be there to help her out because she wouldn't let me drove me insane. I knew I fucked up, but that shouldn't have stopped her from loving me. In fact, nothing had stopped me from being madly head-over-heels in love with her.

In the meantime, I'd been goin' through the motions of life, and kept surfing longer and harder to ignore the fact I woke up without Harper layin' there in my bed. The very scene I would ache to see wasn't there for me, and I didn't think it ever would be again.

I had a lot of time to think about the shit I pulled on Harper, and it was fucked up of me. I shouldn't have done it. I was disrespectin' our relationship, and it wasn't how I should have been actin'. I should have treated Harper like she was the fuckin' queen of my castle. I should have respected her boundaries in our relationship, and I didn't. I was selfish and not thinkin' when I placed my lips anywhere near Kylee's face.

Harper loved being kissed on the forehead. She did this cute little thing with her nose where she would wrinkle it up in order to signal that she wanted to be kissed there.

Shit. I missed those cute little faces she made, and I had no one else to blame but myself.

I put all my frustrations and general pissed off attitude into my surfing. My shit impressed Finn, and tonight he was finally going to treat me to a night out. His exact words were more like:

"Brah, let's go pick up some ladies and get your balls back before they sink farther up into you. Time to celebrate the mad waves you've been taking out there."

Finn was a fuckin' joke, but even he had been acting weird as fuck lately. As much as he jokes around and shit, he kept tiptoeing around me. Probably 'cause he knew before I went to Texas, he over-spoke when his drunk ass told Harper about me going out there with Kylee. I was still pissed about that, but whatever. We were "bros" so it's a 'move on' kinda moment.

The night was already slow, and I dropped Evelyn off at Kylee's, who was surprisingly very abrupt about the whole situation. When I pulled my truck into her driveway to drop off Evelyn, she was already outside waitin' for me.

"Come on, Evie. Let's go. Say goodbye to Daddy." She brushed me off like I wasn't even there.

"Hello to you too, Kylee." I said sarcastically.

"Ryder." She said coolly, while grabbing Evelyn out of her car seat and snatching up her backpack.

"Always a pleasant experience seeing you," I barked.

"I hear you are going out with Finn tonight?" she asked, clearly changing subjects.

"Sure am. What's it to you?" I questioned.

"Oh, just heard you were. Well, good luck." She winked and walked away.

What the fuck? I swear to God I think that chick is fucking crazy. I never understood her when we were married, and I certainly didn't understand a damn thing she said now.

I pulled my truck out of her driveway and drove to the bar where I was meeting Finn. Tryin' to shake what that crazy bitch said, I was focused on getting to the bar and getting a damn beer. I was sick of women constantly fucking with my mind. One second she was rubbing up on me like a cat in heat, and the next, she was all about this new man of hers. Who, I might add, remains a fucking mystery to all.

When I finally pulled up to the bar, I threw the clutch into park and walked into the dive to find Finn sittin' in the corner with two Bud's on the table.

"Hey, bro. What's up?" he shouted over the loud music coming from the DJ booth in the corner.

"Fuckin' Kylee. Crazy motherfuckin' bitch." I was so pissed that I pounded the beer.

Finn surprised me with his reaction; it was weird because his face suddenly turned completely blank. He just sat there drinking his beer silently. I half expected him to agree with me, but he just sat there, so I decided to change the topic, because clearly, he wasn't about the shit-talking.

But hey, that was Finn. Sometimes he could be a real obnoxious piece of shit, and other times, he was all about getting along with everyone. Some kumbaya bullshit, or along those lines, ya know?

"I haven't heard from Harper."

He perked up a little bit, and was glad I had shifted the conversation. Fuckin' weirdo.

" Why don't you go out and find yourself another lady, my man?" Finn asked.

"Because there is no one else for me, dude. When you are in love, there is no one else who can replace the person who is in your every damn thought, and for me, that's Harper."

"Dude, you haven't even tried to mack on any other girls. I think it's time. I have a little competition we should do." Finn's eyes looked mischievous, and I knew the bastard was up to something, but I played along for the sake of continuing the conversation, and providing some sort of entertainment for the night.

"Aight, dude. Lay it on me. Let's play your little fuckin' game," I half-mocked in his accent.

"Okay, don't get feisty now." He laughed but continued with what he was sayin'. "Now, you gotta go pick up the girl of my choosing here. You cannot say no. You gotta buck up and do it. I don't give a fuck about Harper or what she might think because, dude, you're not with her, so you gotta branch out."

This was not what I wanted to do. I wanted to show Harper that I needed her back in my life, not pick up some strange girl. Plus, with the wedding, I learned my lesson that picking up girls doesn't mean that Harper won't stop by at any given moment. And it would kill me for her to see me talking to some chick, when really all I wanted to be doing was talking to her.

"I don't know, man. I think it's a pretty fuckin' stupid idea." I confessed truthfully.

I honestly wasn't into tryin' to pick up other chicks. I wanted one girl in my life, and that girl didn't want me back; so I was going to sit here and wait my entire life if I had to, in order to convince Harper that I needed her in my life.

"Just for shits and giggles." Finn laughed and pounded the rest of his beer. He waved over the waitress, who came bouncing over with her perky round tits popping out of her shirt.

"My buddy here is newly single," he started talking to the attractive waitress, but he kept glancing over at me, "and he needs a couple of your best shots because he needs to loosen the fuck up."

She laughed and started to turn away, but not until Finn stopped her and pulled her back.

"He also needs to grow his balls back and start flirting with some girls. Now, you are a girl; so tell us, which girl in this bar is going to talk to my man Ryder?"

Ah, here was the douchebag-Finn that I knew and fucking loved. I knew this son of a bitch would eventually come out.

The girl just laughed and smiled at me. "He shouldn't have any problems picking up any ladies in the bar here." She winked and walked away to grab our shots that Finn had so graciously ordered for me. What an asshole.

"Come on dude, just one girl. I am not telling you to go over there and sleep with her; just get your juices flowin' a little and go talk to her. There isn't anything wrong with flirting. It never harmed *anyone*," he emphasized, and practically pushed me off my stool.

"Alright, Finn. I'll have one conversation, but after that, I want you off my D, dude. I ain't sleeping with no one, and if the girl is a total bimbo, I am getting the fuck outta there," I announced.

"Yeah buddy!" Finn pounded my fist and started to look around the bar to pick, I am assuming, the hottest chick at the dive.

"Them." I looked to where he was pointing and saw a blonde chick who looked oddly like Kylee, with much bigger and faker tits. I didn't know what Finn's fascination with blondes was, or what his deal with girls lookin' like Kylee was, but I shrugged and walked over there after grabbing the two shots the waitress had just brought over. If he was going to make me flirt with these girls, the least he could do was provide the drinks we were going to drink.

"Hey there," I drawled out, emphasizing my accent that I know girls swoon over. She looked up and giggled emphatically.

"Hey." She smiled and stared up at me.

"Shots?" I asked. I hated this whole forced-flirting thing. It was fuckin' hard, man. Girls had it so easy. Guys would just come up to them and start talking, but dudes had to actually come up with conversation and have the balls to see it through. We had to make sure we didn't sound like self-proclaimed douchebags, but then again, we didn't want to sound like fuckin' pussies either. Guys have to search the situation out and make sure the girls weren't there just to have a girl's night. It was fuckin' hard. Too damn hard to pick up a damn chick.

"Sure." She laughed, and her friends backed away slowly from the table once they realized I was talking to their friend. We drank our shots, and then introduced ourselves to each other.

Turns out, she was a graduate student at one of the local colleges here. Her name was Morgan, and she was born and raised in San Diego. She had recently been divorced, like myself, and had two kids back at home. Her friends had forced her out of the house, sort of like Finn. We actually had a pretty good time talkin', and from where Finn was sittin', it probably looked like we were going to get together. But both of us had this unspoken truth that neither of us was really lookin' to do anything but talk.

After about a half hour or so, what I thought was completely appropriate, I headed back to where Finn was watching the game. I shook her hand, and thanked Morgan for the conversation. It was sort of what I really needed.

I needed to know that women weren't always out there for men, and that I was capable of talking to a woman just to have a conversation with them. It was something I needed to know to convince myself that I couldn't love anyone else but Harper.

There was no one else out there in the world I would have rather been with, except Harper. During Morgan and my conversation, it was nice to talk to someone else, but I couldn't be with anyone else physically or emotionally. I wasn't capable of loving anyone but Harper. I needed her with me all the time, every day. I thought of her constantly. She was the light of my every moment. Finn was just goin' to have to be pissed that I didn't put out. It wasn't for me.

"Dude, did you score?" Finn asked, as I walked over to where he was watching the game.

"No way, man. I told you. There is no one else for me but Harper. She's got herself fuckin' twisted around my heart as fucked up as that sounds."

Finn did something I didn't expect at all. He shook his head and nodded. Before he spoke, he took a sip of his beer.

"I need to tell you something, dude." He knocked off the rest of the beer and waved to the waitress, indicating he wanted another round.

"What's up?" I asked with some concern. There were very few times when I saw Finn serious. Once was when he told me he thought about leaving his good job to surf professionally, and the other was when he told me the story about how his dad died in a surf accident when he was a kid. Other than that, the dude had been the buddy who could make me laugh hysterically. He was never the serious type. Just a buddy.

"Don't freak out, man." His other beer arrived, and it was clear he was starting to feel the buzz of the booze.

"What the fuck?" I asked.

"I need to tell you something about Kylee."

"You know why the bitch was actin' crazy as fuck?" I asked.

"Promise me, dude, that you won't freak out. I have known you for years now. It would be really shitty if what I am about to tell you is going to ruin our friendship. Plus, I want to be able to live so I can kick your ass in the surf competition that's coming up," Finn half-joked.

"You're startin' to act like a goddamn pussy, so tell me what the fuck is goin' on before I walk outta this bar."

"Okay, okay. I am going to start off by telling you the whole story from the beginning. It was the night after all that shit went down with Harper, when I sorta spilled the beans about Texas. Well, when you guys left, my drunk ass stumbled to this smaller classy-ass bar downtown. I recognized Kylee and walked over there, because honestly, I wasn't thinking."

Fuck. I could tell where this goddamn story was going to go already. I was too fuckin' curious to make him stop, but a part of me wanted to beat the shit out of him for consorting with the enemy.

"We talked the entire night. It was fucking crazy. Normally, when I am about-to-pass-out-so-drunk, all my mind keeps doing is thinking about fucking the first pussy that walks by; but all I did with her, and all I *wanted* to do, was to talk. We stayed out until the bars closed, and just walked and talked. She went home, and I passed out at my crib; but the next morning, she was still on my mind. Like, I couldn't shake our conversation and how she made me feel…off; so I decided to give her a call.

"From there, everything just moved so quickly. By the time she had to go to Texas, we were just starting to grow with our relationship. We both decided to be monogamous. We have spent almost every day with each other. I didn't want to step on your toes, though, because I know Evelyn is spending more time with Kylee, and I felt like I had to tell you I was most likely going to be there too."

I felt fuckin' betrayed by this dude. But at the same time, I thought, if Kylee was with Finn, he must have heard about the big blowup; he didn't react like Harper did. There was a part of me that held hope from this fucker's story. Selfish thinkin', I know.

"So, y'all are like a thing then?" I asked.

"Yeah. It's a strange feeling, dude. I never meant to hurt you, or for this to happen. I guess you don't *expect* to fall in love with a girl, but when that feeling takes ahold, there is nothing really you can do about it but ride the wave."

I sat for a second so I could see the little shit squirm in his seat. I totally understood what he said, and I understood the idea of falling in love, and not being able to stop being in love. It's how I have been tryin' to explain to everyone the feelin' I have for Harper.

"This is the same thing I feel for Harper. Now you understand when I say I can't just stop loving her just because she left me. She owns my body, my soul, and my life."

"I get it, dude. I totally get it now. Are we cool?"

I thought about it for a second. I remember how happy and over everything Kylee was at the wedding. It was nice to see Kylee free, so to speak. She looked fuckin' happy, and of course, I knew Finn was a good guy. He was my buddy for fuck's sake.

And around Evelyn? He was amazing. He never disrespected her, and has been around her since she was little. I knew he wasn't going to press being her dad because he respected me as well. I couldn't feel anything but happy for 'em. Honestly. It was really good to see Kylee move on.

"Dude, it's all good. I am happy Kylee is off my dick and onto yours." I laughed—and Finn didn't look too pleased—but continued with what I was tryin' to say.

"Kidding. For real, man, it's all good. We have been friends for too long for this to affect us. I still need my surfing buddy. Plus, when I was in Texas, I saw Kylee and she hinted that she had a new man. She rubs me the wrong fuckin' way, but we never worked out and you know that. If y'all work out, I would be more than happy. Plus, you're amazing around Evelyn. There is nothing really more I could ask for in a partner from her. I'm glad you came to tell me, honestly."

"I was worried as fuck dude." He hesitated, then laughed a nervous laugh.

"You weren't mad when I kissed Kylee on the forehead for that photo? I know you know about that, because not only have I complained, but I'm sure Kylee said something."

Finn stopped for a second, then said, "No dude. I totally understood where it was coming from. You wanted a moment to show Evelyn what a family unit looked like, because Evelyn will never get that. She will always come from a crazy family of step-mothers, half-siblings and her parents. I understood where you were coming from."

"We are being such pussies about this, dude." I got off my stool and gave him a hug. If we were being such girls about this, we might as well close the deal with a hug.

"I love you, man," Finn said, half joking.

When I sat back down, I said, "Now you know, though, why I can't be with anyone else. There isn't anyone else out there for me. Maybe what I realized from this whole damn thing is that Harper is mine. Forever and Always."

"Go get her, Ryder. Seriously, stop moping around this joint and go get her. Shit, stalk her if you have to. Go to her place and wait for her if she won't pick up. Then make your case. She has to feel the same way. I know she has to. There is no one else out there for her, but you."

"Your right, dude." I started picking up my things and shovin' 'em in my pockets.

"Wait, you're not even going to finish the game?" Finn asked.

"No time. I gotta go get my woman back," I said and walked out of the bar.

I needed my Harper here with me, now. I needed to show her that she was my everything, and I would never do anything to intentionally hurt her. Everything Finn said was right. Kylee was happy with Finn, and that moment we shared was so that Evelyn could see what her original family unit looked like for one second.

I got in the truck and drove straight to Harper's house.

Chapter 14

Harper

"What do you want?" I asked when I picked up the phone. What the hell would Kylee want? She wanted to ruin our non-existent relationship more? Fuck that bitch. Did she want to shove it in my face that she was back together with Ryder?

"Harper, please don't hang up," she blurted.

"What do you want, Kylee? Seriously. You freaking ruined my relationship, now you want to taunt me with it? I am not dealing with this." I was about to click the phone off when I heard Kylee's hesitant hiccup of a sob.

Kylee? A human being with feelings? Is that at all possible? It couldn't be! Kylee was a self-consumed little bitch is what she was. A bitch who wanted Ryder more than she wanted any other guy on this planet. *Ugh!*

But alas, something told me to stay on the phone and continue listening. Maybe she had something valuable to add to the conversation, and the fact that she was getting all emotional about it really drove home for me.

"Harper, I swear to God, I never meant to hurt you. I admit, in the past, I wanted Ryder back. But that wasn't my intention at the wedding. My intention was the same as his. In fact, I was…well, listen. Would you mind meeting me in person? I have a lot to say, and I promise I won't chew you out or anything. I really just want to explain my story."

What would be the benefit of meeting this bitch in person? She just admitted she wanted Ryder in the past. A part of me knew I shouldn't meet with her, but another part of me was curious. There was always that little innate side to ourselves that forced curiosity through our blood. I wanted to know what she had to say to the "other woman".

Was she going to bite my head off, or was she actually interested in telling her side of the story? I knew deep down inside that I should just move on from this, but the fact that I kept thinking about Ryder, the fact that I…touched myself thinking of him, flicked something in my brain to recognize that I wasn't over him completely. Maybe Kylee could shed some light into who he was as a person, and what his intentions were. Meeting with Kylee would either emphasize what I already knew, that Ryder was a no good piece of shit; or she would tell me something I didn't know.

Sure, I was secretly hoping that she would tell me Ryder was perfect and wonderful, that this feeling I had for him, she never did. All of that was just a shot in the dark though. I really expected her to tell me Ryder was an ass, but shit, my damn curiosity got the best of me. I was just going to meet her in a public place, and make sure that Skye and I had something planned so that I could run to her after the meeting was over.

"Okay. But I am only staying for a little bit," I finally said.

"No problem!" She replied, all too bubbly and excited. She probably had no idea that I would say yes.

"Text me when and where, and we will go from there."

"Sure! Let's plan on next Thursday. That's when Ry…um, that is when Evelyn will be at her dad's," she corrected herself, as if the thought of hearing his name was going to get me all anxious.

"Yeah, see you then, Kylee." I hung up and immediately dialed Skye's number.

"Hey, bitch!" She answered with her usual greeting.

"Oh my God. You will never guess who just called me?"

"Who?" Skye asked.

"Kylee. Freaking KYLEE!" I almost screamed over the phone.

"Ew. What did she want?"

"She wanted to meet up with me. Something about talking about what happened."

"What did you say?" Skye asked.

"I said yes. I mean, I am so freakin' curious about what she has to say to me. She has never once wanted to talk about it, and hell, maybe it will provide some sort of closure, ya know?"

"When is the meeting?" Skye asked without any sort of emotion in her question.

"Thursday. I was wondering if maybe you wanted to meet up afterwards?" I asked hesitantly.

"Absolutely, babe. Gotta go to class. See you then." Skye air kissed over the phone and quickly hung up. Strange, but that was Skye: a big weirdo.

***

A few days passed and it was finally Thursday. We were going to meet at this little chain coffee shop in the middle of La Jolla. I wanted to meet her in public and not over a meal so that I had an excuse to leave. Afterwards, I was meeting Skye at a boutique to shop for her wedding dress. That only left me like a half hour with Kylee.

My palms were so sweaty, but I think as I processed this meeting throughout the week, I realized that I had nothing to be worried about. In fact, I was the one in control of the conversation, and anything I didn't want to say did not have to be said.

I saw her walk in with her perfectly curve-hugging yellow sundress and oversized sunglasses. Her hair was a sun-kissed blonde and brushed to the side. She had a small bow on the left side of her hair where it held together some loose strands. She looked glamorous in a completely unintentional way. Most girls would envy such beauty…including myself.

I watched her walk over towards me, and that's when I really felt my heart pick up and start racing. I was suddenly super nervous to meet with her and hear what she had to say. But as quickly as she walked in, I found myself faced with her sitting in front of me.

"I see you already ordered a coffee. I'll be right back," Kylee said, her voice laced with a seductive-like whisper.

I watched her walk over to the coffee stand, and saw her standing there getting a drink. She walked gracefully, with determination and ease. She ordered her drink, paid the barista, and sauntered back over to the table.

"Thanks for meeting me," she said, while taking off her sunglasses and sticking them on top of her head.

She took a sip of coffee and stared at me, expecting a response. I couldn't respond, so I just sat there looking at her, waiting for her to continue with whatever she had to talk about. After a few moments, I think she got the hint, and continued with what she was going to say.

"I know this is totally awkward for you, but I wanted to pull you aside to tell you about what happened at the wedding. I am so sorry, Harper. If I did anything, it wasn't my intention—"

"Other than sleep in the same bed as Ryder…" I mumbled gruffly.

"I am so sorry, seriously. I was drunk, and that wasn't my intention at all. I brought you here today to show you that I am involved with someone else. I am seeing someone, and I am falling in love, so I get how you feel. I understand how hurt you must have felt when you saw me, Ryder, and Evie together. Honestly, it was nothing. It is so hard for little Evie to grow up without her parents together. She constantly asks me why Mom and Dad don't live together, and why she always has to travel between houses. It really hurts to tell my daughter that Mommy and Daddy don't love each other like that. How do you explain that to a little girl?"

I sighed, because for a moment, I felt sorry for Kylee.

"I just wanted a picture that would capture a complete family for Evelyn. Who knows what the future will bring, ya know? I just wanted that memory, and I think that's what Ry wanted too."

I shuddered when she said Ry; the familiar nickname bothered me with a tinge of jealousy.

"So, seriously. I never met to do any of that. I was stupid, and this is effecting my new relationship as well. I am trying to make amends here."

"I understand, Kylee, but there is a part of me that feels broken when I remember Ryder kissing you on the very spot that he kissed me in a romantic way. I remember you kissing him before we even got together. I just can't shake it." I confessed truthfully.

"That was the old Kylee, Harper. Love does crazy things to some people, and I have fallen head-over-heels in love with Finn…"

"Wait a second. Finn? As in Ryder's Finn?" I asked, baffled.

"Yes, him."

"Does Ryder know?" I asked.

"Yeah, Finn told him last night. When I dropped Evelyn off at Ryder's house today, we talked about it. He is cool about the whole thing, surprisingly."

"Well, wow. Congrats, I guess, are in order." I was stunned. I never expected such an upidty Kylee to get together with surfer-dude Finn, but hey, they say opposites attract.

"I guess this has got me thinking. I can't stop thinking about him, Kylee. You know that weird butterfly feeling you get when you see Finn? That's how I feel about Ryder. I know you guys didn't work out, but does that mean we won't?"

"Harper, we didn't work out because we weren't compatible. The only reason Ryder was with other women when we were together is because, honestly, I was a huge bitch to him. I sort of forced our relationship, and it was so wrong of me. I felt so bad once I realized how love actually felt; it suddenly allowed me to realize how fucked up I used to think when I was with Ryder. There was nothing good about us together. Nothing."

I was about to say something, when Kylee continued.

"Listen, I know how much Ryder talks about you. He does it with me, and I saw him, and he looks absolutely miserable without you. He hasn't been going out; and he just sits there with Evelyn, going through the motions, but you can see how absolutely depressed he is. There is nothing good about this separation, Harper. I would love nothing more than to see you guys together with a future."

It took me a while, but I realized how hard this must be for Kylee. To tell the "other woman" that it was okay to date her ex-husband and the father of her child—it took some balls on her part, and I appreciated it. I knew we weren't going to start any Brady Bunch ordeal, but the fact she was pushing me to Ryder said something. It made me believe that maybe Ryder was actually the one for me, that I made a gross mistake.

It wouldn't make any sense to call him now, though. Talk about embarrassing. I have too much pride. After everything that happened with Tye and my past, I feel like I have built up this independent persona around me. I couldn't make the first move with Ryder. It would be too much of a kick to my ego. I know I sound so whiny, but it really is something that means a lot to me. I just don't think I have it in me to make that first move and confess that I was wrong. Call me stubborn. It's just something that's part of my personality.

"Thanks, Kylee. I appreciate it. It's been a long journey with Ryder and everything. Please know that I would never cross any lines with you and your daughter. I actually really appreciate you meeting with me."

"So, are you going to call him?" Kylee inquired.

"I don't think so, but who knows? I have to go now. Sorry. Thanks, again," I said, and started getting up to go. I didn't want to be late meeting Skye, and quite frankly, this conversation was just too intense for me. I was sort of overthinking all of this. Kind of like the numb feeling. I was trying to numb out any emotion I felt that was creeping to the surface about Ryder.

"He really misses you, Harper," she said, getting up and surprising me with a hug.

I was not a hugger. In fact, the only person I let hug me was Ryder and Skye. It was something about that close intimacy with someone that I couldn't stand.

I just kind of curled up and patted her on the back, and walked away, saying goodbye. I walked to the car and drove over to the bridal salon, where Skye was probably harassing the poor sales lady about dresses.

It was a weird sensation. On one hand, I felt sort of relieved that Ryder's intentions were always with me, but I still felt uneasy about the whole situation. I was irked that Ryder would even do those things. He should have pushed Kylee away when she snuck in bed, and he could have not kissed her on the forehead and gotten the same family photo effect.

But there was another side of me that loved that crazy stupid man. We all make mistakes, it just matters what the impact those mistakes make on lives that counts. Is it really worth this crazy fight/break up we are having? Honestly, probably not.

But like I said, I have way too much pride to even bring this up to him. I couldn't. There is absolutely no way.

When I pulled up to the bridal salon, I walked inside to see Skye harassing the sales lady about how sample sizes should come in different sizes besides size 0.

"Skye, play nice," I called.

"Harper! So glad you are here." She came over in a beautiful, poufy, tulle wedding gown, and kissed me on the cheek. She looked absolutely stunning. The corset on top hugged her curves like a second skin, and the bottom poofed out like a fairy tale princess's dress.

"Wow! Skye Monroe. You look freaking amazing." I was completely speechless.

"This gross thing? Ick. I hate it. It's too much dress for me. I want something classier. I was *trying*..." she emphasized, while staring at the poor sales lady who was probably shaking in her boots, "to tell this lady that I wanted something with a little more class, and a less prom dress look."

I walked around the store for a few moments and started picking up different dresses for Skye while she argued with the sales lady. I started running my hands over the beautiful white and off-white dresses. They were absolutely gorgeous.

Secretly, I had dreamed about my wedding since I was a kid. I always wanted a big white dress to walk down the aisle in. I had always imagined my father walking me down the aisle, although now, I'm not too sure. With everything that happened with Tye, I don't even know if he would consider coming to my wedding…

Anyways, I had always imagined walking down a long lined aisle, and looking at my future husband's face at the end of the aisle. I imagined the look on his face, the smile that would spread ear-to-ear. I could already feel the way his hand would feel when he would take me from my father. That spark that we would share in that brief moment would be a testament to our undying love.

I could imagine his eyes staring into mine as we hold hands and the officiator goes on about staying true and faithful to each other. I pictured it almost like a movie. Where everyone is talking around us, but we are there sitting in our own moment. We are there as one, sharing that moment and holding each other close. Our wedding would be the most flawless event that I would ever plan because, as a Type-A personality, I know I would have everything down to the very last flower petal.

And the sad part?

Those eyes I pictured are pools of sparkling blue. Those hands I touched are big strong ex-football player's hands. Those moments we shared are only with him. Ryder. My one true and only love.

I knew I messed up. I couldn't stop thinking about him. In fact, the wedding I seriously have dreamt about since I was a young child included him. When I was younger, the face always changed as I grew, from Ken doll and GI Joe, to Matthew McConaughey, all taking the place of the groom. But now, all I could think about was Ryder. This whole wedding was just pulling on my damn heartstrings. Of course I wanted this for myself. I would be ignorant to say that I haven't secretly hoped I could find my Prince Charming and walk into the sunset all happy-go-lucky.

But I guess that lifestyle wasn't for me. It wasn't in the works for me. I was always going to be that girl who lived in the reality of today. There was no bright future or exciting romance planned out for me. I was average, and had to deal with the pain of a breakup just like everyone else who has gone through something like this. It was just something I had to go through, and I chalk today up as a weak day.

I snapped out of my thoughts and picked up a dress I knew Skye would immediately fall in love with. It was a mermaid-style dress and puffed out where the knees were. It had some lace on the top, and thin straps that were wrapped with lace too. It was the epitome of a stereotypical classy wedding gown and perfect for Skye.

I brought it to the saleslady, who had driven Skye back into the dressing room, and was clearly frantic, trying to find the perfect dress, but was struggling.

"Here, bring this in and have her try it on." I gave the dress to the lady, and walked over to the sitting area where a very attractive server gave me a glass of champagne. I could hear squeals coming from the dressing room and immediately knew I had done well.

After a few moments, I heard the daintiest footsteps come clamoring in from the back.

"ERMAGOD." Skye was able to squeak out when she saw herself in the mirror.

"I just died over this dress." She looked at me, waiting for my approval.

"And guess whose best friend picked it out for you?"

"You did not?!" she half-asked and half-yelled.

"I did too."

"I love you so much, Harper Mae. You just get me," Skye said.

"You look stunning babe." I got up to go give her a hug, and she got down from the pedestal and wrapped her arms around me.

"Don't get makeup on this dress, because I am buying it," she squeaked, and we both fell into a fit of giggles.

"Seriously, this is amazing."

"So," I asked, "are you saying yes to this dress?" I asked.

"Yes! Absolutely," she cried, and ran back to the dressing room to change. I downed the rest of the champagne and sat back down to wait for her, not letting my thoughts wonder anywhere else.

Once Skye came back in casual clothes, she grabbed my hand, dragged me out of the store, and down the street to her car.

"Hop in, homeslice," she demanded.

"What is going on?" I asked nervously.

"Don't question it."

"What happened to the dress?" I asked her.

"Oh, it is going to be altered. It's a process, Harper Mae, and the wedding isn't for a while," she said, getting into the driver's side.

"Where are we going? You know my car is, like, parked right there." I pointed just up the road to her.

"I know, but you are not driving. I am." She was being super shady, and it was bothering me. I knew she was up to something. She never acted like this.

"What is going on?" I asked again, more annoyed.

"You know how much I love you, right?" she asked, pausing as if she was waiting for an answer from me.

"Yeah, I mean, we have been friends for so long. I would hope at this point you love me," I batted my eyelashes at her" to try to act goofy because she was being super serious.

"I am trying to be for real, Harper. You know I do everything *for* you, and not because I am trying to *hurt* you, right?"

"Sure. You're seriously starting to freak me out though. Can you please tell me what is going on?" I asked, shifting in my seat.

I looked outside my window, and saw the familiar road down Genesee, which led to my apartment complex, that we took quite often.

"Are we headed to my place?" I questioned again.

"I cannot tell you where we are headed. Well, I guess I could. Yeah, we are going to your place, but I need you to remember that everything I do is for your sake. You know that, right?"

"Sure, Skye. You're acting like a crazed mad-woman right now, but sure, I know that. I do the same, ya know? I would do anything for our friendship," I said.

"Good, just remember that…" she mumbled off, saying something completely inaudible.

"Are you…sweating?" I provoked.

"Shut up, biotch. Yes, I am sweating. You don't need to point it out. How embarrassing."

"What the…fuck is going on?" I was seriously so confused. We were pulling closer and closer to my apartment. This was so weird; if she wanted to go to my place, she should have just let me drive home and then followed me or something. Now she was being all twitchy.

I swear, it must've been a full moon because everyone was in full crazy-mode. First, Kylee wanted to meet with me, and not only that, but she was actually nice to me. I was shocked that I even decided to meet her. Skye picked out a wedding dress, and it was surprisingly much easier than I had anticipated, because she is so freaking high maintenance. Now, Skye is acting like the Mad Hatter and driving to my apartment while sweating profusely from her armpits.

What.

Is.

Going.

On?!

Once we got to my complex, Skye pulled into a guest parking spot and shoved the shifter into park.

"Are you going to tell me what is going on now?"

"Nope," she said very quickly. How strange. A moment ago at the bridal salon, she was so excited and full of energy. Now, she is sitting here with a very serious look on her face.

"Is there a bridesmaid's gift inside?" I questioned.

"I wish this was a gift."

"Okay…so are we going to go inside, or what?" I asked, because the curiosity was getting the best of me. I wanted to see what the heck the big deal was.

"Okay." She took a deep breath and reached for the handle to open the door.

"Now, remember what you said earlier. Repeat it to me," she told me.

"That I love you?" I inquired.

"Yeah, say it again," she demanded.

"Okay, I swear. No matter what happens, you will remain my best friend, and I love you, so..." I said to appease her nerves, which were obviously out of control.

"Can we go inside now?" I asked again.

"Yeah, I suppose we should go." She pulled on the handle and walked outside. I followed her up the steps to my door.

Skye looked like she was about to pass out. She was white in the face, and her palms were glistening from the sweat.

"Girl, you are starting to scare me," I said, but put the key into the doorknob and opened up.

I was still staring back at the freaked out Skye, who looked like she saw a ghost when I opened the door. I lightly laughed, but turned around to see what she was gasping about.

My heart sped up a hundred miles a minute.

My hands dropped my keys to the floor.

My throat was immediately dry.

My stomach was doing a hundred different somersaults.

I was queasy, nervous, excited, and felt like I was dreaming or in another world. There was no way Ryder could be sitting in my living room.

Absolutely.

No.

Way.

Not Possible.

What the hell was Ryder Andrew Kent doing sitting in my living room as if he lived here and owned the place? Sure, I gave him a key when we were dating, and had planned on getting it back, but I just hadn't felt like seeing him. I didn't think that he would ever actually use it like this.

And Skye…what a fucking cunt. Seriously, I was so pissed at her. Now, it was all very clear that she had been a participant in all of this. This was some sort of a sick joke on her behalf. She had no right to sit here and orchestrate all of this. This wasn't her life she was fucking around with, it was mine. MINE, damnit!

"You are such a bitch," I spat at her, as she followed me inside and closed the door behind her.

"I told you to remember what you said. Harper, I am so sorry, but there really was no other way to get him here. He sat me down this morning and talked to me all about it. He told me everything that happened, and you should really hear him out." Skye tried to talk as fast as she could as she followed me into my kitchen, but I pushed her away and grabbed for a glass so I could pour some water into it. At this point, I hadn't even given any sort of acknowledgement that Ryder was there.

When I poured my glass of water, I felt him come up next to Skye, so I violently turned around and faced both of them. As I held the glass up to my lips and downed the water, I stared at Ryder in the eyes, not even blinking. There was nothing in that stare but pure unadulterated hate. The same hate I felt for him when I saw the kiss with Kylee.

See, I knew I was right. I didn't have feelings for him. I hated him. Ugh. I knew it. I should have never tricked myself into thinking that it was possible to trust him again. There was no love left between us. We were broken.

Both of them stood there in stunned silence as I finished my glass of water and stuck the cup in the sink. It was so silent that you could hear a pin drop from miles away. When I finally spoke, it was like I was screaming from the top of a mountain, but really my voice was barely above a whisper.

"What are you doing here," was all I could croak out. There were no other words for him being here.

"Harper, please," he began, but I was too disgusted with all of this to listen.

"No. No. Absolutely not. This is unacceptable." I huffed and stormed into the living room. I had no idea what I was doing, but I tried to look busy to avoid the rampant thoughts that were flooding my brain.

I didn't let either of them talk before I continued with my train of thought, "And you, Skye? Why would you do this? I am your best friend. You are supposed to be on my side. I don't care what he does. First off, you are not supposed to meet my EX-boyfriend behind my back, no matter what. Second, you didn't tell me about that meeting and then told him that it was acceptable for him to show up to my home. The place where I find solace and peace. You thought it was totally okay for him to just show up here. What did you think was going to happen? He was just going to apologize and I was going to drop down to his feet? Fuck that!" I screamed at her.

She came over to me with tears falling down her face. Ryder attempted to come with her, but she pushed him back to where he was standing, looking stupid in the corner by the kitchen.

Skye approached me with ease, but when she got next to me, she pulled me to the couch to sit down. When we were sitting together, tears rolling down her face, she took her hand and tucked a small strand of hair behind my ears.

"Harper, I told you that I loved you and wouldn't do anything to ever hurt you. You are my very best friend, and I meant that. You are like a sister to me, and everything I did with Ryder, I swear, I had you in mind. I wanted him to come here so you guys could hash it out. All I have seen you do is be miserable without him. There was no way I could have just sat back and allowed you to continue stumbling down this road of misery."

She continued after pausing to wipe a tear from her cheek, "I saw you hurting yourself, and when I went to meet with him, I had all intentions of yelling at him too. But then I saw that same hurt in him, and I knew you guys were just too stubborn to admit that both of you were wrong. He was wrong for doing that with Kylee, and you were wrong in terms of telling him and yourself that you aren't in love with him. I saw you today at the bridal salon, fuming over those wedding gowns. I have seen your Pintrest wedding board. There is no denying that you want a wonderful wedding, and a man like I have. And there is no denying that you want it all with Ryder. So stop being so fucking stubborn, and just hear him out."

She looked at Ryder, who was staring hopefully at me.

"Both of you need to hear each other out. When and if this is all over, and if there is no coming to a compromise, then you both can at least say you tried. There is no harm in trying. At least then, you can move on with your lives, because you guys are stuck at this impasse with no direction of knowing where to go."

She was right. I either needed this closure, or I needed to realize that Ryder was doing it all for me. She also was correct in assuming that everything I did these past couple of weeks was because I missed Ryder. The reason I stayed at home alone was because I missed Ryder. The reason I met with Kylee was because of him. Everything I did, he still consumed my thoughts. So I owed it to myself to hear what he had to say at the very least.

And I knew it wasn't her fault. I was just being dramatic. Skye was looking out for me, and I was punishing her for that. Never once had Skye done something with malicious intentions. She was right. And she technically prepped me in the car, I was just too naïve to realize what was actually happening.

"I know. You're right." I could see Ryder out the corner of my eye sigh a deep breath of relief, so I made it a point to correct what I was saying.

"Skye, you are right. Not you." I directed at Ryder, whose shoulders immediately tensed up again.

"I know you would never do anything to hurt me, so there has to be a reason that you're doing this now. I will sit and listen to what he has to say, but that doesn't mean we will get back together. You're right, though; we do need to talk. The way Ryder and I ended things wasn't the right way. Thank you for doing this."

Skye had finally stopped crying, and we both hugged each other again. I was truly thankful for her in ways she will never know. We could be oceans apart, but she was always going to be my best friend. When I was with Tye, there were days when I wished I had a friend like her, and I am so grateful for everything she has done for me now. I wished we had met earlier in life, but there was always a rhyme and reason for why some people come into your life when they do.

I needed Skye to help guide me in the right direction and excuse my stubbornness, which is what she was doing now. I loved her like I would have loved a sister. She was a sister for me, and I knew I was going to be the best bridesmaid for her that I could be.

"I love you, girl," I whispered in her ear when we embraced.

"Love you too, you stubborn mule," she joked.

When we finally parted, she spoke up, "Okay, I am going to go now, but you guys sit down and talk."

She patted the seat next to her indicating for the very quiet Ryder to go sit down. When she got up, she gave me two thumbs up and walked out of the apartment, closing the door behind me.

I guess it was time to finally face whatever came next.

***

"So, go on and speak." I said angrily. My mood instantly changing from something positive to something more along the lines of annoyance.

"Harper, I just need you to listen. Can you do that for me? Can I please say what I have to say without you interrupting?" He was so nervous, that it was kind of cute.

He was clearly shaking in his shoes, and man, he looked so incredibly handsome. He was wearing a pair of leather shoes, with a dark pair of designer jeans, and a grey and white flannel shirt. The shirt he wore showed off in the bulge of his chest because it was tight around his abs. His pecs were staunch. You could see the definition of his abs and it had me practically drooling. Then, of course, there was his gorgeously square jawline that was cut perfectly so that his cheeks almost looked contoured to his face.

He was grinding his teeth, but tried to smile at me when I looked up at him. It was almost like he was walking on a tightrope, and with each step he moved closer to me. His black hair was slicked back, but a few strands fell onto his forehead. I stared down and noticed his large arms were shaking underneath him, but it was from the fists he was making so hard it's like he had a death grip on something, maybe his nerves.

He was sporting his light stubble on his face, which looked so incredibly sexy on him. It didn't look disheveled on him, but more like a, "oh yes, fuck me, please" sort of face. And that's what got me to his baby blues.

His eyes were glistening pools of shimmering blue. It was almost as if I felt like I was in a boat on the ocean, just staring out at the horizon with nothing else in sight. It was a very calming thought. It was as if I was drifting on the ocean alone, just floating and dreaming. When I stared at his eyes, there was nothing and no one else in the world. That's the part that scared me about Ryder too.

When I looked at him, I felt momentarily at peace, like everything in the world was slowing down around us and he was there to protect me. He was going to save me from the crazies in the world that seemed to flock to me. He was there to protect me, hold me, and cherish me. That was what I felt by just staring at him. That's why I demanded that when we broke up, we didn't see each other. I knew this would happen the moment I just looked at him in his eyes. He had this effect on me.

Sure, I saw women surround him at bars and clubs, but none of them felt the connection, the spark, that we felt for each other. He never looked at them the way he looked at me. He was never like that with them, just with me.

So, did I owe it to him to sit here and listen to him? I mean, I don't think I did, but the sole fact he was staring at me with his sad little puppy dog eyes forced me to nod at him while he sat down next to me.

He turned his body so he was facing me, and very slowly and carefully, he put his hands on my knees. He looked as if he was going to cry any second. It was heartbreaking to watch. I felt like I was disappointing him, almost, by not being with him. He loved me, and I think I was starting to realize I messed up by rushing to conclusions and leaving.

Therefore, I sat. I sat there and waited to hear what he had to say. And that's when he began.

Chapter 15

Ryder

"Baby, I am so sorry for everything you saw. I acted like an ass the entire trip and did everything possible wrong. It started when I was bookin' the trip. I wanted to see Knox get married and all, but I was bein' a dick. Babe, I should have invited you from the start. I didn't think..."

"I guessed you weren't interested, and I didn't wanna take you back there because I don't have a lot of fond memories of Texas. Going to see my parents was the hardest damn thing I've ever done. I didn't want anyone to think I was a fuckin' pussy, but I was a mess when I went to their house. This sounds stupid as hell, but I wanted their approval. I wanted my dad to say that everythin' was gonna be fine, that the past was forgiven and that he could move on with our lives. Part of me knew that would never happen."

"It's fuckin' embarrassingto come from a family that doesn't want a damn thing to do with you. I'm ashamed that you would think I'm a useless piece of shit, and that's what I feel like when I'm there. That's the reason I don't ever go back. They make me feel like utter shit. I work for my money and I worked damn hard at my football career, all I've ever wanted was for them to be proud of me. I ache for it. Secretly, I hoped that when I showed up at their house that they'd welcome me with open arms. They'd be over the fact that I ain't in law school and be okay with my choices. But, in the end they weren't and I think I'm finally okay with that, because in the end game I'm okay in life. I've got that surf competition comin' up and I'm pretty damn excited about it."

I heard her pretty little angelic voice start to interrupt, so I looked back up at her from where I was staring at my fingers. She looked so beautiful. Her face was contorted in some sort of anger, but it was soft, like she was listenin' and payin' attention to my story.

"When is the competition?" she squeaked.

"October. In a few weeks, actually."

"Oh. I'm excited to come watch," she said.

Those words made my heart skip a beat, and I wanted to tell her more and more of my story. I wanted to share, and bare my entire soul to her, so I continued with what I was sayin' previously.

"Yeah, so that's why I didn't want you comin' in the first place to Texas. I'm embarrassed with everything that involves my parents. Of course, like they always fuckin' do, they tore me down and make things involving them a livin' hell. They don't ever plan on comin' to visit me or ever seein' their own goddamn granddaughter. I started thinkin' what kind of grandparent I would be with Evelyn's kids and what kind of dad I am to her. First, I thought maybe I was like them, but I'm nothin' like that sperm and egg donor I got stuck with. Evelyn is always first in my life. I think I just needed to realize that so I could move on with my life."

"At first, I thought I needed their approval to be a good parent and later on down the road, a good husband to you but I finally realize I don't. I don't need a damn thing from them. They're fuckin' dead to me and I don't need their goddamn approval. In life, there are just people that will never approve. It fuckin' sucks that it's my parents, but I don't give a shit at this point. I needed to go there and say what I had to say. But once I was done, I was done with them. All I need now is to move on with my life. I have a beautiful daughter that I need to prove to that I am nothing like her worthless grandparents."

"And I needed to know what kind of a man I was goin' to be to you. Was I going to end up like my father, who used my mother as arm candy? Was I just using you as a social excuse to move forward? No. But, that's what I had used Kylee for. I used Kylee to make my family and the rest of society happy. It was so fuckin' hard to come from a wealthy neighborhood where everyone cared about keepin' up apperances. It wasn't just for the girls either, the guys had to be groomed to become their fathers. It was all who you knew and how much money y'alls family had. Of course that's how I felt our relationship was. I never wanted to grow up in a neighborhood like that and I damn didn't want my wife and kids to be surrounded in that shit."

"Did I freak out? Fuck yeah. I was scared, but I grew from my closure I had from them. I shut that door tight, and I don't wanna open it again. I'm over it. Done. Been there. Don't care to go back. Kylee feels the same way as me, so it was nice that she decided that she didn't wanna move out there. I was freakin' the fuck out when I thought she was actually considerin' draggin' our daughter out to Texas to live forever. That's part of the reason I'm okay with her and Finn datin'..."

I paused for effect to see whether or not I knew she knew about this tidbit, but she didn't move or blink, so I continued.

"Finn's keepin' her here, and I am just glad that she found someone, and feels the way I feel when I speak to you or think about you. Anyway, I'm getting off subject. I want you know exactly what happened. When we went out as a pre-wedding celebration thing to one of Knox's clubs, I got shit faced. Just bein' in Texas was sendin' me back into a depression and I needed an out. I stupidly used alcohol. I had a moment there where I thought I could live this life, but I would be a fuckin' miserable alcoholic who would be doin' a borin' ass nine-to-five job.

"So, I continued drinkin' till I got blackout-drunk. I didn't know Kylee had slipped in my bed until it was too late. I had felt so fuckin' guilty about it all; I was trippin'. I called you right away; I swear to God, Harper. I didn't let one second pass without givin' ya a call. I felt so fuckin' guilty baby. I promise you it had nothing to do with me. I will never get blackout-drunk again..."

I started to continue with what I was sayin', but she stopped me.

"It's okay, Ry. I believe you," she whispered out, like my little angel she was, in such a sweet tone that broke my fuckin' heart in two.

"Please forgive me," I begged.

"I do. I promise."

"But I'm not done. I need to apologize for bein' a stupid, fuck–face, douchebag prick at the wedding. I wasn't thinking then either. I was all caught up in the moment. I know Kylee told me she was going to go see you and talk about all of what happened. I didn't agree, but she pushed it, so I know you heard Kylee's reasoning. And I have to admit, if I agree with her on anything, it would be that."

"I never meant to hurt you like I did, Harper. I really just wanted a family photo. Something to put up on the wall before stepparents, stepsiblings, and all that jazz came into the picture. Honestly, I was thinking about marrying you right then and there when I got back to California. I just wanted that moment with Evelyn and Kylee before shit started bouncing off the walls. I wanted to share it with them..."

She interrupted, "I know. I am so stupid. Goddamn it, Ryder. I feel so silly, like a little girl who got stuck in a lie or something. I don't know how else to explain it. I just...I don't know. I totally see it that way now. I was acting completely irrational. I don't know why I didn't think of asking you first."

"But, Harper, you broke my heart when you fucked me in the hotel. I came back there, begging to tell my story, but you broke my heart. I knew it was over. I have never cried in front of a girl until I met you. Well, besides when Evelyn was born. I knew it was over with you though, and my heart felt like it was bein' torn in two. When we fucked that night, it was different. Man, I am going to sound like such a little bitch for sayin' this, but it's like we were makin' love or some corny shit like that."

Harper laughed hysterically, then wrinkled her little nose up and snorted, which made me laugh. She was the cutest thing around.

"Anyway, I didn't know what to do without you. I just sat there in my house as if I was expecting you to come back and sit with me. I wanted to see your naked little ass running back and forth from the bathroom to the bed because you just got out of the freezing cold shower. I missed naked cooking, and cuddling together. I missed you, damnit."

"What I am tryin' to say with all this is that I don't want to live another moment, another second, without you in my life. I need you. I breathe you. You own my every thought, my soul, my heart, and my body. You are a part of who I am."

"Oh, Ryder." Harper had tears in her eyes, which broke my heart even more. All I wanted to do was protect her from all the pain in the world.

I walked over to her and did something that even surprised me.

Chapter 16

Harper

He hugged me. He pulled me tight into his arms, and hugged the crap out of me. I grabbed him and pulled him deeper into my arms. I was wrong. I was a stubborn mule who clearly was too high-maintenance for my own good. I needed to get ahold of my emotions because they were getting the best of me.

I protected my heart because that's what my past told me to do. I thought, *protect it, otherwise you'll be in a vulnerable situation that might lead to going to jail, or some other crazy shit.* That's why I learned to run away. I thought I fixed it too, but I guess I didn't. I needed to know that Ryder was here to save me, not hurt me. He really is my knight in shining armor, no matter how corny that sounds.

"I'm sorry," was all I could say.

I knew this was quick and abrupt, but I knew I was wrong. It was not right for me to push Ryder away just because of my own insecurities. I knew the criticism I might get from someone watching this scenario, and I don't care what they have to say. Sometimes, you just know when you're wrong and you fix the problem. In this case, I was completely and totally in the wrong. I hurt Ryder in a way that's unexplainable. He cried over *me.* Over *me!*

How could I have ever stooped to such a low level that someone would cry over me because of what I did? I felt awful about myself. This wasn't who I wanted to turn out to be. Ryder talking about his family got me thinking about my own. I didn't want to end up like my family either, who pushed their daughter away when their daughter needed them the most. But, that's exactly what I was doing to Ryder. I was pushing him away when we needed each other the most. He was my one and only. There was no more pushing or shoving. He was mine and here to stay.

"I love you. This is all my fault, really," I told him with tears exploding from my eyes.

"I'm nothing without you, Harper. You own me in every way imaginable." He whispered seductively in my ear, then pulled me even tighter against him if that was even possible.

We were smushed together like a sandwich on the couch. I was crying, and he was holding me close. I hadn't imagined this day would turn out like this, but I wouldn't have traded it for anything. This is who we were, stuck together forever.

He slowly pulled my face towards his, and lightly pressed his lips against mine. I felt like I was being touched for the first time. The electricity shot through my core and sent shockwaves of delight dancing through my body. I was electrified by his touch. And just like that, I pulled his face in deeper, more passionately, as our tongues began to explore.

Just as he pulled in, he pulled away.

"I love you, Harper Mae. Please tell me you'll be mine…forever."

There was really no good way to answer that but with one short word.

"Always."

I loved this man more than I could tell you, more than I could speak. It didn't make sense, but I just knew I did. Shit, I was going to have to call Skye and tell her all of this. I needed to apologize to her again. She was right, and I'm so glad she forced me to sit down and listen to her, because I wouldn't trade this moment for anything. I immediately made a mental note to call her tomorrow and apologize for being a total bitch to her.

"Baby?" Ryder asked hesitantly.

"Yeah," I responded.

"I love you."

And those three words determined our future. A future we were going to have together.

I pushed my way towards him, and shoved him back on the couch, meeting my lips with his again. I felt the velvety moistness of his touch as I caressed his lips with mine. It was so amazing to feel his actual body instead of imagining it in my head.

I blushed and Ryder looked at me puzzled.

"What's wrong, babe?" he asked.

"I was just thinking of something embarrassing," I confessed.

"What is it? Tell me." He started to sit up straight, but my arms pushed him back down.

"When we were on our break," I paused, turning red in the cheeks from imagining how I was going to say this.

"Well?" he questioned when my pause extended.

"When we were on our break, I just...kind of...decided one day that I missed you. I missed your touch, so I closed my eyes, and imagined you touching me."

He looked completely puzzled.

"I started to...you know? Well, I started to touch myself...down there." I stumbled over my words, not able to get it all to come out.

"You masturbated?!" Ryder looked completely shocked. It was so abnormal for me to do something like that so I shocked him. He rolled onto the floor, unaware of how to react to the whole situation.

"I don't know what's so shocking." I huffed, getting down on the floor to push him because I was angry that his mouth was still open wide.

"No, baby. No, no. I am shocked because you got so red over that. I think it's fuckin' sexy. You have nothing to be embarrassed about, so don't worry!" He continued chuckling to himself, but pulled me onto his lap. I wrapped my legs around his torso, and we sat there on the floor where I was fake–pouting, and he had the biggest smile that spread from ear-to-ear.

"I think it's super sexy actually." He said, taking my lip between his and biting down slowly.

Once again, we were at it. Our lips did our typical dance, shooting electric shocks down through me. But I was hungry, and craving more. I needed to feel him against me.

I slowly pulled off his shirt and rubbed my hands down his abs. Yes, this was definitely better than imaging them. This man was mine…all mine, and I had him here with me. I felt a swelling in my center and knew immediately I needed to touch him deeper, further, and more passionately. I raked my fingernails down his chest, leaving a trail of red marks, but this only made him moan.

"Oh baby, you wanna play rough?" he mused.

Grabbing my ass, he got up from the floor and carried me to the bedroom. He threw me onto the bed, which excited and surprised me. I was anxious and nervous to see what he had in store. He threw himself on top of me and let his erection in his pants rub against me as he kissed me ferociously.

I groaned in pleasure and thrust my tongue deeper into the depths of his mouth, exploring ferociously. He gently moved his hands to pull off my shirt, which exposed my simple black lace bra. Thankfully, I decided to wear one of my push up bras today.

I looked up at him, and a seductive smile danced across his face. He was so turned on, and we both were trying desperately to continue with this foreplay, but we were in dire need of the main event. We were hungry for each other, but Ryder just rubbed his jeans against my bare thighs, grinding into me. We were dry-humping each other, as I took my ankles and put them behind his back, locking them in place. I needed more of this game we were playing. This wasn't enough.

I moved his hands down closer to the hem of my shorts, and pushed them down into my panties. He was a little shocked at the bluntness of the moving, but he obliged. I wanted to surprise him. I wanted to give him something that he didn't expect.

"Wait here." I stopped him, and he looked completely puzzled.

Poor guy probably thought he was getting blue balls, but little did he know…

I ran to my closet and pulled something out of a box in the back. Then I proceeded to scoot my boot to the kitchen and pulled something out from the refrigerator. I ran back into the bedroom and stared mischievously at my man.

"What do you have there, my love?" he asked with an arched brow.

I threw the handcuffs to him, and the whipped cream that I pulled out, and seductively prowled my way up towards him.

"Oh. Fuck," he growled and grabbed me, thrusting my hands above my head.

He slipped one cuff over my left hand, and then closed the other cuff over my right. My hands were trapped above my head, and it felt so incredibly sexy to give him the control. I wanted him to be my master tonight.

"Oh yeah, baby. You will be mine tonight."

He grabbed my hips and pulled me down towards the edge of the bed. He pulled off my bra and slipped off the rest of his clothes. He was standing there in all his glory. His body was that of a walking god. That's where he grabbed the can of whipped cream and opened it. He continued to stare at me with his ice blue eyes, deep into my soul. As the cap popped off, he started shaking the bottle.

Then he slowly lowered the tip of the nozzle between my breasts.

"I'll be taking this off," he said matter-of-factly, pointing to my bra.

He unclasped the front hook and pulled it off quickly, letting my perky tits bounce free.

That is when I felt the cool, moist fluff pour onto my nipples. I heard the swirling sound of the whipped cream, looked down, and saw the trail he painted. Each breast was covered, and there was a slight trail that went from the top of my tits down the middle of my stomach.

He proceeded to unbutton my shorts and pulled them off, taking my underwear with him. He continued putting whipped cream on me, covering me all the way down to my center with whipped cream.

"Mmm, baby. I think I am craving some whipped cream. Can I lick this off you?" he asked, while slicking his tongue around his lips as if he was salivating at the sight of me tied up and covered in whipped cream.

"Please," I begged.

He pulled his lips down onto my left breast and circled his tongue around the whipped cream, licking it desperately. He flicked his tongue around them, nibbling down slightly. He then followed the trail he created for himself, which lead to the other breast. This time he grabbed my other tit and massaged it furiously while he licked my breast clean.

"Mmmm. God, I have never wanted to eat whipped cream more in my life," he moaned.

Once he was finished around my breasts, he moved down the trail he painted onto my belly. He followed slowly, taking each lick of his tongue, but leaving some whipped cream behind. Once he got to the top of my pussy, he licked all around my labia before he dove in.

His mouth felt extra moist and creamy, and his tongue continued to dive deep into me. I loved watching his face as he licked me up, paying very close attention to my body's reactions.

I was sticky from the whipped cream, and the handcuffs were still on me. I wanted to take a bath, but I secretly loved the fact he was sitting there basking in my stickiness.

He started to move his fingers around my clit while he licked me clean. Once he finished, he slid up towards me and looked me dead in the eye.

"You are such a bad girl, Harper. I am going to fuck you now."

With that, he shoved himself inside of me, slamming against the walls and my clit, making me cry out for more. His large cock was repeatedly moving quickly in and out of me, and all I could think about was trying to remain quiet because the neighbors were going to think I was being murdered.

But, I couldn't hold it in. So I howled as he pushed deeper inside of me, swallowing me whole. We were two sticky lovers attached together in a pool of sweat and sex. I loved watching his cock ride my pussy as he moved in and out in a quick motion, shoving him fully inside of me.

I loved how he felt as he lightly tapped my g-spot, making me wetter as time went on. I wanted to grab onto him but I was handcuffed above me, so he grabbed my hips and threw himself inside of me desperately. Grinding deeply, I felt the pressure built up.

"Get. These. Off. Me," I demanded, pointing at the handcuffs. I was trying furiously to get rid of them because I needed to grab onto something. I wanted to rip my fingernails into Ryder's back, and ride his cock until I was numb.

He pulled the handcuffs off me with the key that was sitting on the nightstand. I grabbed onto his rock solid abdomen and flipped us around so I was riding his dick. I moved my hips hard into his so that I could feel him all the way inside of me. I gasped in surprise at the full thickness I felt, but continued moving deeper onto him.

He grabbed my hips again and helped me move in a repetitive motion that resembled the waves crashing into the shore. That's when I felt that sudden need to explode. I was close to coming, and I needed to experience this with him. I wanted him here with me so that we were doing this together.

I gave him a look and he immediately understood what I wanted from him. So, he dove deeper inside of me, and I rode faster, waiting for both of us to detonate like a bomb going off.

"Oh yes," he groaned.

"Now, baby. I need it now," I begged over and over again, until we both were on the same wavelength and the pressure inside of us burst through.

I felt him ripping the largest orgasm out of me. The warmth of him spilled all over me as I growled and released my own orgasm onto him. I cried out in pleasure with his response following a second behind. I crawled off of him, laying down next to him, and felt the warm wetness leak out of me.

It was a glorifying feeling to experience the most intimate pleasure that a person could ever feel. Certainly, this was the kinkiest sex I have ever had to explore. When I was finally able to feel my legs, I got up to go wipe myself off. I found Ryder curled up in my bed, under the covers, and patting on the other side for me to join him.

He was exhausted. No, we were exhausted; but this was the part of sex I really and truly enjoyed more than anything else. That time we got to sit there curled up next to each other, just holding each other. I could taste him there, and feel the sweat on his skin. We were still sticky from the whipped cream, but neither of us really cared at this point. All we cared about was that at this moment, we were present with each other. And in this moment. We were there, together. Always and forever.

Chapter 17

Ryder

I loved her. Three little words would describe everything I felt for Harper Mae. If I could, I would give her the whole world. In fact, I might die tryin' to give it to her if that's what she wanted.

"I love you so much, Ryder. Please don't ever leave me again. I don't want this fighting anymore. I want our happily ever after," she begged.

I couldn't see her face because it was dark, but I knew she was sitting there smiling contently just by the way she was clinging' onto me. I pulled her in tighter to make sure she understood that I wasn't going anywhere. I was never going to let her go again.

"I'll never leave you ever, Harper. I need you to trust me. I need you to really trust me, okay?"

"I promise. I'm done running, Ryder. Every time we run, we always seem to find a way back to each other," she said in the pitch black.

"I know, baby. I know."

It was silent for a second. I just couldn't believe this is where we ended up. I was so fucking nervous comin' over here. Skye had called me and came up with this complicated ass plan, but she was convinced it would help me get Harper back. I had my doubts man. I really fuckin' had my doubts, but it all seemed to work out for the best.

I thought for sure Harper was going to freak the fuck out and run away. I was expecting her to slap me a couple times, but none of that happened. She was thinking about me too on our break, and that's what really got me pushin' for her.

When Skye left, I thought she was just going to keep interuptin' my speech that I worked so hard to plan out, but she didn't. She let me talk and listened. She gave a shit, and that's all I wanted from her. I wanted her to listen and hear me out.

Suddenly, I heard some rustling of the sheets and felt that she had moved her sweet little body so that she was facing me in the dark. With her tits pressed up against my chest, I couldn't keep my dick from getting hard. The fuckin' thing had its own brain. But then I heard a small little voice come out of her mouth and I knew immediately what she was goin' to say, and it was going to be tough for her to get out. I took my fingers and trailed them through her hair, just tryin' to remind her that I was here for her.

"What baby?" I asked.

"Can I tell you something?"

"Anything," I told her.

"I will pick up the pieces of your past and steal your heart forever, Ryder." She whispered delicately in my ear.

This made my heart drop.

I knew what I had to do.

***

It was well past three o'clock in the morning, and I still hadn't gotten a second of sleep. I was furiously researching on my phone while Harper lay knocked-the-fuck-out next to me. It was beautiful listening to her sleep and watching her chest rise and fall with every breath. I couldn't wait to make her mine forever.

I took my arm, put my chest to her back, and breathed her in. The sweet smell of flowers and woman wafted into my nose. There was no other way to describe the delicate smell that Harper seemed to always have. She was so fuckin' perfect to me, even little things like down to the smell of her body.

I closed my eyes for a little bit and waited until my alarm woke me up at seven in the mornin'. When it finally did, I was fuckin' anxious and nervous as shit, but more excited. I knew what I had to do, and what I'd have to do to get it done. I also knew that Harper liked to sleep in on Saturdays, so the likelihood of her waking up before eleven was slim to none. I needed to get outta here before she did, otherwise it would've been 100 questions that I didn't have answers to. I wrote her a note just in case she woke up, tellin' her I went out to the ocean. I told her that when she woke up, she should go over to my place. This had to be done at my place, by the ocean.

When I hopped in the truck, I went to the place I never thought I'd step in: the mall. Boy, was I on a mission too. I had to navigate this fuckin' place first. It was packed already at this hour, which was ridiculous. I hated shoppin'. I'm glad Harper was all over that, because I wasn't. I wanted nothing to do with it.

I finally found the store I wanted and walked in. My hands were sweating like a damn idiot, but all I kept thinkin' about was Harper in my head.

My baby.

My love.

Mine.

She owned every piece of me, and this was just a way of saying that she did. Nothin' but a damn formality is all. I was so excited that we were finally doin' this. It was time. Finally, it was time.

Some bitch who had far too much pep in her step this morning came over and greeted me with an obnoxious ass smile on her face.

"Can I help you, sir?" she asked.

"Yeah…"

The question was could she really help me? Was I really ready to do this again? The first time I had done it was a fuckin' shame. A damn mistake, really. That wasn't love. It was not even close to what I felt for my baby. My girl.

She was up there with Evelyn. No other woman in my life was at that level. No other would. She was my partner in crime, my cowgirl. She was the other piece to my heart. I would do everything to protect my girls. They were everything to me.

Could this lady help me then? Hell yeah. I was so fuckin' unprepared for this, but it was the best decision I had ever come up with.

I knew the moment I saw Harper laying there in bed, curled up against me. The heat of her body kept mine warm, and her sexy legs wrapped in mine. It was at that moment that I knew everything I worked for in my life was for this. She was my number one supporter. She loved me as an ex-football playing surfer who worked at a damn coffee shop.

I couldn't describe how I felt for her. The fact these thoughts are even crossing my head feels so stupid as it is. I feel like a big-ass pansy doin' this, but I wanted to process this again. This was going to be the beginning of the end.

'Course, I was ready to answer her questions and 'course, I knew what the answer was.

"Yeah, you can. I'm looking for engagement rings."

Chapter 18

Harper

I missed him in the morning. I was curling up in the sheets of my bed and he wasn't there. I saw the note he left for me on the stand and knew he would be gone until early afternoon. Poor baby must have been nervous for the upcoming surf competition. It was his first big competition since he stopped playing football.

It was nice, though. I basked in the silence and familiarity of his scent in bed. I sighed. I started to get up and hop in the shower before I headed over to his place. I wondered why he wanted me to meet him over there, but I'm sure he had something planned since it was our first day back together as a couple. Secretly, I was hoping for some extravagant dinner or something that we could share between the two of us, but I would be okay with just ordering Chinese and sitting and watching movies. Although I doubted there would be much movie watching going on.

Man, was I a lucky girl? A stupid girl who thought she knew everything, but really knew nothing. A girl who thought that pushing people away would protect her. Really, it was all about finding the right person to share your heart with. That person was one-hundred percent Ryder. There was no doubt in my heart or mind.

We had been through so many obstacles that were put up to tear us down, and nothing could keep us apart. We were bound for and to each other. When we were together *we* only existed. I was stupid, but I coughed it up to learning from mistakes. I wasn't going to run anymore. It was my turn to settle down.

At first, I didn't think I believed that I could settle down. I didn't think it was possible for someone with so much baggage to do that; but finally, with Ryder's help, I was able to believe.

I believed that I was a person who deserved to be loved, and love in return. I was a person who was allowed to open her heart up to love, and that someone could love me with all their heart right back. It scared me; there was no doubt about that. But, now I know it's completely possible to be in love and to have someone love you.

Once I got out of the shower, I put on a light sundress and grabbed my bag. I packed an overnight bag because I knew I was probably going to end up staying at Ryder's for the night. Ah, it was so good to say that. I loved his house. It made me feel so comfortable and at home. The house itself was beautiful, but what really made it a home were the people inside of it.

I couldn't wait to see Evelyn. I hadn't seen her in weeks and I missed her. Just like I loved Ryder, I loved little Evie. And what with Kylee being okay with our relationship, I felt a little more comfortable. I was hopeful that we all would be able to create some sort of stable family system for her. Sure, it wasn't going to be your typical family, but we would love her just as much. Probably even more because there were more of us for her.

Once I got in the car, I felt something shift in the air. The sun shone a little brighter, and the world felt a little easier to live in. I knew I had to call Skye, so I made a mental note to call her while I waited for Ryder at his house. I hummed a familiar tune and drove all the way to his house.

This was going to be the first day of our life together. I can just picture it. It just made sense. There was no one else.

I loved Ryder Andrew Kent with every bone in my body. Always and Forever.

Chapter 19

Ryder

When I got back to the house, I saw her sitting there on the phone talkin' to who I assumed was Skye by the way she was chatting.

"No, I totally get it, babe. Yeah, I know you were just doing it all for me. Seriously, I still love you. Stop it; you're being ridiculous. Of course you're my best friend, and I would love to continue being your maid of honor."

When she saw me come in, a smile crossed her face. I was so fuckin' nervous, and she hadn't a clue why. That's why it made it even more nerve-wracking. She had absolutely no idea what was about to happen in four short hours.

I knew I wanted to wait until sunset. All that romantic bullshit, ya know?

"Skye, I gotta go. Ryder just came in the door. Yeah, I'll call you tomorrow. Love you," she said, and hung up the phone.

She got off the couch and ran to me, gripping me in a bear hug.

"Hello, handsome," she said, laying her plump lips on me.

Was I a lucky guy, or what? I had the most amazing woman in the world, and she wanted to fuck me all the time. I couldn't wait to spend the rest of my life fuckin' her senseless.

"Want to go run some errands?" I said, tryin' to get my fuckin' mind off what I was going to do.

"Sure!" she exclaimed.

We spent the rest of the day picking up groceries and other things for the house. It was a few hours of just being with each other. Stupid little errands that would define our future together.

When we got back, I realized it was 4:30pm. I wanted to take her outside to watch the sunset, so I grabbed a blanket, and hurried her outside.

"Get a sweatshirt," I demanded.

She ran and got one of my sweaters from my room and put it on. She looked so adorable because the thing was way too big for her, but somehow she pulled it off. She could pull off wearing anything, but if it was mine, she looked incredibly sexy in it. I'd rather see her come down here naked, with her ass out. Oh man…

Shake it off, bro, I tried to tell myself, and saw her bolting outta the back door. God. This woman here was goin' to be mine for the rest of my life. This was goin' to be my wife. The stepmother to my little girl, and the woman in my life. She was my forever. Always.

We sat down in the middle of the beach, but no one was around us. I knew she got embarrassed with PDA so I tried to pick somewhere private.

"What are we doing out here, baby?" she asked sweetly.

"I just wanted to sit out here with you. It's going to be fall soon, so we won't be doin' this much too often. Can't a man want to spend time with his love?" I told her.

I was fucking sweating from my palms. I didn't want to touch her because the minute she felt the sweat, she would know something was up. I had the ring tucked away in the inside pocket of the jacket I was wearing. I tried to position her around my lap so there was no way she felt it. I just hoped she didn't try to undress me 'cause there was no way I could resist her, but I didn't want to ruin the plan.

There ain't much of a plan though. I just figured I'd know when the time was right. It was right before it got dark outside, and I'd just ask her. Nothing really special about it. Simple and sweet. Just like my baby.

"Well, that is awfully romantic of you, Ryder," she half-joked.

"I am a sap. Don't tell the boys." I laughed.

"It's beautiful out here, isn't it?" She was staring straight into the ocean. Her back was pressed against my right side and I propped myself up on my elbows. I would be her pillow any day of the week willingly.

"Yeah. It's beautiful in fall," I said honestly.

"I miss the changing seasons sometimes though. In Chicago, it would be almost snowing right now. Well, maybe not snowing, but it would be way too cold to be doing this," she said.

She spoke beautifully. I could hear her talk all day long. God, I was just so fuckin' sappy right now. I don't know what got into me. *Snap out of it, dude. Get your fuckin' balls back, bro.*

It was the nerves. Fuckin' nervous. I had to get this shit over with. There was no more postponing it. I needed to just ask her. I looked at the sunset, and it was perfect. They called it 'the golden hour' out here by the surfers. Perfect time to finish your last wave before heading home.

"Babe, can you turn around and look at me?" I asked her.

She positioned herself up and around so she was sitting cross-legged, but looking right at me. The golden sun was shining behind her hair and she looked like a goddess. Her brown hair was shimmering in the light, and her eyes were perfect. Those big brown eyes. The eyes I'd stare into until I was old and grey.

"What's up?" she asked.

I started fumbling. I should have planned this shit out better. I had no idea what to do, or where to go from here. All I could do was speak from the bottom of my heart. That's all I had for Harper, my heart.

"You know I love you more than anything, right?" I told her.

"You are starting to sound like Skye right now," she half-joked.

"I feel like I have answered this a hundred times in the last couple days, but yes, I do. I know, and I love you too, Ryder," she continued.

"Harper, I'm bein' all serious right now, so will you just listen to me?" I was aggravated with her. I was trying to say something, and she was totally crampin' my style.

"I'm serious!" she barked. "Go on; I'm listening."

"Harper, you know I love you more than anything. I love you more than all the stars in the sky. I love you more than all the clouds on a cloudy day, and the wind in the rain. I love you more each day. I want you to grow with me. I want you to be with me for the rest of my life."

I was fuckin' shakin'. My hands had no clue what the fuck they were doin'. It was like they were just chillin' there. I placed 'em on my knees and sat cross-legged facin' Harper, but it felt and looked uncomfortable as shit.

"I love you too, Ryder. Seriously. I love you more than anything. I would give you the world. I promise, I am done running. I trust you. You know how hard it is for me to trust someone, and I trust you. You own every piece of me as well. I do everything with you in mind. I would never do anything to hurt you…ever."

She was perfect. Just perfect.

I grabbed into my pocket and stood up. I looked at her, and watched the shock on her face as she noticed I had a little black box sitting in my hand.

"Will you please stand up?" I asked her.

If I couldn't plan the whole what-I-was-going-to-say thing, then the least I could do was plan this. I wanted to make sure this part was perfect.

"I will love you more than the waves in the ocean. I promise you this. Always and forever, Harper Mae. I will love you forever and ever."

This was the truth. We were forever. No matter what. It would always be us.

Chapter 20

Harper

And then he got down on one knee.

***

***

Epilogue

She was sitting there. I saw her in the magazine.

Her.

Harper.

My Harper. Sitting in a fucking magazine cover with some pussy-ass bitch. He looked like a fucking douchebag. Who the fuck stops playing football, then surfs. But at least now I know where she ran off to.

She will be mine again.

I can't believe she ran off without me. She is a useless little piece of shit. That bitch thinks she can run away without me, and get me in trouble? Hell no.

I grabbed my computer and found the first plane ticket to San Diego. I grabbed one of the credit cards I stole from the rager the other day. I hoped it would go through before the owner cancelled the card. I needed to get to San Diego to her before she could run away again.

She had to be punished for her crime. She had to be mine again. Did Harper really think she could run away from me? I only had trouble trying to find where she was. She was never really gone. I thought about her all the time.

She was always on my mind, and she needed to know that. I needed to show her that this…man she was with, was no man at all. He would never take care of her like I did. He was a piece of shit. He was useless. I would be the only one she ever needed.

I found the cheapest ticket and booked it for a month from now. I had to prepare. I needed to get some stuff so that she would come back home to me. She needed to come back home to me. She was MINE.

I threw the computer against the wall, getting irritated reading the article. I should never have been on that stupid sports website. I knew I shouldn't have, but I am so glad I found the article. I am so glad I found my baby.

I ran to pick the computer back up and there were a hundred little cracks in the top right corner, but I could still make out the picture on the screen.

There she was with her beautiful brown hair, which was longer than I remembered. It's okay; when she came back home, she would fix it. I needed her like my baby. She would have to fix it.

She had those big brown eyes I remember staring in. Those brown eyes that said yes to everything I told her to do. She was the only one in this world that actually listened to me. I knew I should have taken the blame for everything that went down, but it wasn't my fault. See? I needed her with me. She did everything for me, and she just up and left me.

She left me standing there, looking like a motherfucking idiot at the courthouse. She couldn't have the last say. That was for me. I wanted the last word. I wanted to give her the closure she needed.

I needed revenge.

I needed to plot.

God, she made me so fucking mad. How could the same girl infuriate me to the point of exhaustion, and at the same time, make me want her more than I have ever wanted anyone in my life. I couldn't wait to have her back in my life. That piece of shit that has her now is only a temporary holder. He is just warming her up for the main course: me.

I couldn't wait to see the look on her face when I showed up. I couldn't wait to be there with her again. I would bring her back to Chicago, no matter what it took. She needed to come back home with me because her home was here. She didn't belong with that other man.

And if he got in the way? I didn't care. I would kill him before he stood in the way of me getting my girl back.

She would be mine again.

Soon baby. I am coming to get you, soon enough.

Dear Reader,

Thank you so much for reading and loving my second novel! If you would please leave me some feedback and reviews wherever you purchased this item, that would be much appreciated. Indie authors thrive on our reviews!

I am working very hard on finishing novel number three. I have a few projects in-between that I want to get to that I promise are as juicy as this.

I hope this isn't too much of a cliffhanger for you. If you want to keep up with me, turn a couple of pages and check out how you can.

To the endless indie author community, thank you for allowing me to join and connect.

Peace, Love, & Happiness,

V

Acknowledgements

First and foremost, I want to thank my parents and family for helping me and supporting me through this novel. Although it may seem at times that this will not be a career or something serious, I love you all very much for supporting me through this time. You understand and realize how much this means to me and I could not thank you enough.

Second, I want to thank all the fans, supporters, friends and bloggers for helping me with the success of my first novel. Without you I would not have topped Amazon and Barnes & Noble's charts. I would not have become a worldwide bestselling author. For you all, I am so grateful.

I also want to make sure I thank all my amazing author friends and the huge indie community. You all have been a huge support and amazing to me. Thank you especially to Jake Bonsignore and Danielle Jamie who have been there for me even through pestering emails and annoying messages. Thank you guys so much!

Danielle, um, you are my rock. I am so thrilled to have been able to meet you this year in Las Vegas. Um…ice machine room much?! I love you so much and am so grateful for everything you have done. You are my author best friend always!

Taylor, thank you for being my rock and support. Thank you for helping me through this novel and life in general. How can I thank someone for being so awesome? All I can say is that you will always be there for me and for that I am forever grateful. Also, Rita's shop is pretty on cue, huh?

Kayla the Bibliophile. Thank you so much for working on editing my novel for me. Thank you for letting me use your blog as a homebase and support and for your hilarious video snapchats, which I should respond more to. Again, for all those annoying messages, I apologize but seriously, you rock.

My assistant, Ashley. ERRRMAAAGOD. Where would my brain be without you. You have the most amazing notes ever….no really. You keep me completely sane and grounded. You help run my blog, my page and pretty much my life. Thank you for supporting me through this and hopefully I can work with you in the future ☺

To the rest of my beta readers: Danielle, Amy, Jennifer, Jessi, Dianela, Chantel you guys are awesome. Thank you for providing AMAZING feedback to me. I wouldn't be here without you!

Thank you to my friends who have heard about this too many times to count. To my awesome cover photographer Liz, author photographer, Cal and models Erin and Bryan. Thank you guys for providing a visual realm for my imagination. Erin, I love you like a sis!

To those who I am sure I have forgotten, to all the incredible bloggers and the online indie community thank you guys so much. To all the groups that have allowed me to post my links you guys are awesome! Thanks for helping me spread the word!

Last, but definitely not least. Jordan. Where do I even begin? When I first came out here, I didn't expect to find my very own Ryder, but I did. Here you are now and I am so excited to go on this adventure with you together. I miss you so much and know that soon we will be back together. I know you are proud of me right now and just know I am so proud of you too, babe. I love you more than all the waves in the ocean, always and forever. Thank you for being there for me.

About the Author

Hi! I am V. Murphy and I love everything about reading (some may call me a bibliophile). I am a current graduate from the University of Illinois Urbana-Champaign with my bachelors in psychology and heading out west to live the California dream while pursuing my Master's degree in School Counseling at the University of San Diego. You can find me writing in a Panera, small coffee shop or on campus. When I am not spending my time in school or reading, I love to write, bake and shop. Thank you for taking your time to pick up and read my story. I hope you loved it as much as I have loved writing it for you. If you would like to know more about me and the books in progress, look me up on the 'net.

Facebook: www.facebook.com/VMurphyAuthor
Twitter: www.twitter.com/vmurphy16
Email: vmmurphy4@gmail.com
Goodreads: http://www.goodreads.com/author/show/4336642.V_Murphy

Made in the USA
Charleston, SC
01 December 2013